A ghost of Christmas past . . .

"Todd, I'd better go," Elizabeth said apologetically.

But he wouldn't let her leave. His arms were around her waist, and he tightened them.

Looking up at him in surprise, Elizabeth repeated, "Todd—please. I'd better go after Tom."

But Todd merely looked down at her. "Liz, for God's sake, one lousy dance. Is that too much to ask? Watts can wait. Don't you get it? I love you. I've always loved you, I will always love you. When are you going to admit you feel the same way?" He tightened his grip on her still further, pressing his body against hers from shoulder to knee.

"No, Todd!" Elizabeth cried, pushing against him. "Tom is my boyfriend now, and Alexandra is your girlfriend! Now, let me go!" Around them people were staring, watching their struggle.

Bantam Books in the Sweet Valley University series.
Ask your bookseller for the books you have missed.

And don't miss these Sweet Valley
University Thriller Editions:

SWEET VALLEY UNIVERSITY®

Home for Christmas

Written by
Laurie John

Created by
FRANCINE PASCAL

BANTAM BOOKS
NEW YORK · TORONTO · LONDON · SYDNEY · AUCKLAND

RL 6, age 12 and up

HOME FOR CHRISTMAS
A Bantam Book / December 1994

*Sweet Valley High and Sweet Valley University
are registered trademarks of Francine Pascal
Conceived by Francine Pascal
Produced by Daniel Weiss Associates, Inc.
33 West 17th Street
New York, NY 10011*

*All rights reserved.
Copyright © 1994 by Francine Pascal.
Cover art copyright © 1994 by Daniel Weiss Associates, Inc.
No part of this book may be reproduced or transmitted
in any form or by any means, electronic or mechanical,
including photocopying, recording, or by any information
storage and retrieval system, without permission in
writing from the publisher.
For information address: Bantam Books*

*If you purchased this book without a cover you should be aware
that this book is stolen property. It was reported as "unsold and
destroyed" to the publisher and neither the author nor the publisher has received any payment for this "stripped book."*

ISBN: 0-553-56653-9

Published simultaneously in the United States and Canada

*Bantam Books are published by Bantam Books, a division of Bantam
Doubleday Dell Publishing Group, Inc. Its trademark, consisting of the
words "Bantam Books" and the portrayal of a rooster, is Registered in
U.S. Patent and Trademark Office and in other countries. Marca
Registrada. Bantam Books, 1540 Broadway, New York, New York 10036.*

PRINTED IN THE UNITED STATES OF AMERICA

OPM   0 9 8 7 6 5

To Briana Ferris Adler

Chapter One

Why am I lying here? Steven Wakefield wondered groggily. With an effort he forced his eyes open to stare uncomprehendingly at a dingy ceiling. He felt as though his head weighed a hundred pounds as he slowly tried to turn it to one side.

I'm in Mike's kitchen, he realized. Vague images of himself helping Mike with dinner, helping him clean the apartment, came back to him as he lay on the floor. *This is ridiculous. Get up, Steven,* he thought impatiently. One hand stretched out to pull himself up, but he just barely touched the leg of the old-fashioned porcelain sink. His hand flopped to the ground.

His head rolled heavily to the other side, and Steven was looking right at the small apartment-sized stove. He stared woozily at it, forcing his eyes to focus. *That smell* . . . The air around him was filled with a sickly-sweet odor, making his nose wrinkle and his eyes tear up. He felt incredibly

1

tired. His body, where he lay on the floor, felt icy cold and weirdly lifeless.

Focus. Above him, impossibly far away, one of the gas dials was turned on high, but no white-tipped blue flame was burning. *Damn.* The room must be full of gas—he had been breathing it. *Have I been unconscious?* He kept blinking to clear his eyes.

Wearily, wanting only to sleep, he tried to call for Mike. A tiny part of his mind knew he must be suffocating, knew that he was losing consciousness. But it was hard to care.

"Mike . . ." It came out as a croaked whisper. His lips were dry, his tongue felt swollen.

In the middle of the ceiling above him, the overhead light swirled dizzily. Pretty blue wavy lines radiated from it, making it look like a carnival light. Steven smiled. Around his head, blue and red points of light danced through the air. Steven sensed pain at the back of his head, but the pain was far away, as if it belonged to another person. He closed his eyes. It was just too hard to keep them open any longer. Now the gas smell was almost pleasant to him—he started to enjoy it. It almost smelled like a room full of heavily scented flowers. His nose wrinkled again. Flowers that had been sprayed with bug killer.

Steven frowned, then pried open his eyes. "Mike," he mumbled. From far away he heard the hiss of canned applause from the TV. He heard Mike's laughter.

Mike, Steven thought hazily. A thin ribbon of panic began to wind its way through his chest. Mike McAllery was Steven's ex–brother-in-law. He was also paralyzed from the waist down—and therefore dependent on Steven. *I have to get him out of here.* He strained to hear Mike in the other room, but no sound could pierce the thick fog surrounding his head. His eyes were open, staring glassily upward, but all he saw were swirling splashes of color, as if a thousand camera flashes were going off in his face. And then nothing—blackness.

"Tom, quit it," Elizabeth Wakefield hissed, trying to squirm out of his embrace. She tried to look stern, but couldn't help giggling as Tom Watts kissed her neck. "Stop it," she said weakly, closing her blue-green eyes and turning away. A cascade of long golden-blond hair brushed across Tom's face. She turned to him again, a rueful expression in her eyes. "We have to study," she reminded him.

"OK," he murmured, brushing her hair back over her shoulder. "Let's study human biology." A wicked glint filled his eyes, and he grinned unrepentantly at her.

Sighing, Elizabeth looked around to see if anyone was watching them. The library was pretty empty—most students at Sweet Valley University had better ways to spend their evenings than being stuck inside the library with a bunch of textbooks for company.

3

"To-o-o-mmm," Elizabeth said patiently. She sat up and tugged her sweatshirt down into place. "*I* need to study for my *lit* class." She grinned. "You could always go study human biology by yourself, in your dorm room."

Tom winced. "Whoa. Cold." He renewed his attack, stroking one finger down her arm.

Elizabeth swallowed, feeling shaky. It was scary, what his touch could do to her, what it made her want to do to him. Quickly she shook her head and took a deep breath, then looked at the open textbook in front of her.

It was ridiculous, and they both knew it. When they were apart, they ached endlessly to be together. When they were together, they were never together enough. Wherever they were, whatever they were doing, they had to be touching, close, next to each other, holding on. It was embarrassing.

Even here in the library, where they'd both taken a vow of silence and concentration, they couldn't keep their hands or eyes off each other. And they hadn't even been here a full hour yet! But every time Elizabeth began reading, she thought of something she wanted to tell Tom. Every time he began taking notes, he dropped his hand to her thigh and rested it there. Every few minutes they had to stop for a moment to kiss, as though if they didn't, they would die. It was getting to be a real pain, Elizabeth thought. It was also getting a little frightening, this obsession she had for Tom. Was this what real love was like?

4

She smiled, meeting Tom's eyes again. She knew that wherever they went on campus, eyes were rolling; yet inside she was beaming, glowing, delirious with happiness. Classes? They sleepwalked through them. Homework? They only went through the motions. This was a new kind of existence for Elizabeth, who had always been the perfect student: diligent, honest, hardworking. But these last couple of weeks she had been intoxicated, stumbling drunk with love.

But that wasn't the only important thing about college life, she reminded herself sternly. There were such things as grades, exams, grade-point averages . . . "You know finals are only a few days away," Elizabeth said to Tom.

"I know," Tom said, gazing into her eyes.

Her eyes were drawn irresistibly to his lips, as though she could taste them even now. "We're in trouble," she said softly.

"I *know*," Tom groaned.

"I need to study," Elizabeth said, pulling away. "But when I'm with you, I can't study."

Tom frowned. "I know. It's the same for me. But what can we do about it? When I'm not with you, I go crazy. Anyway—" He suddenly grinned. "Aren't we having fun, though?"

"It won't be fun when we get our grades back at the end of the semester," Elizabeth said somberly. She fumbled absentmindedly with an envelope she was using as a bookmark in her English textbook. "Who's going to tell my parents I flunked out of college after my first semester?"

Tom moved his chair closer to hers. "I'll write you a note: 'Dear Mr. and Mrs. Wakefield, please excuse Elizabeth for failing all her courses. She's been really busy lately, making out with me in the library. Yours truly, Tom Watts.'"

Elizabeth blushed and shook her head. "Very funny."

"Don't look so serious!" Tom laughed. "I mean, for once in your life you're not at the top of your class, not making a four-point-oh. It's not the end of the world. Of course you should want to spend time with me instead of studying. After all, I did save your life," he concluded smugly.

Elizabeth gave him a playful shove. "Get real, Tom Watts. If you think I love you out of *gratitude*, you have another thing coming."

Tom made a face of mock surprise. "It's not gratitude for rescuing you from that psycho William White?" He looked puzzled. "What is it, then?" He smirked. "My natural good looks?"

Heaving a sigh of exaggerated patience, Elizabeth searched the ceiling for her answer. "Uh, no."

"No? How about my keen intelligence?"

"No, not exactly." Elizabeth bit back a smile.

"My charm? My money? No—scratch that. No money. Uh, my fabulous taste in clothes?" He gestured down to his worn football jersey and faded blue jeans.

Elizabeth looked him in the eye. "Actually,"

6

she said innocently, placing a hand lightly on his chest, "to tell you the truth, all I'm after is your body."

"Baby, you got it," Tom breathed, leaning over to pull her into a kiss.

What the hell is taking Wakefield so long? Mike thought tiredly. *How long can it take to wash a few dishes?* Because Steven Wakefield had been partly to blame for the shooting accident that had caused Mike's paralysis, he'd been sentenced to help Mike with his recovery. It had been mildly amusing, these last few weeks, seeing how much Mike could torture the brother of the woman Mike loved: Jessica Wakefield.

Oh, Jessica. Sleepily Mike slid farther down on the couch. The TV hummed brightly in front of him, but it was hard to distinguish the voices. Then a news announcer came on and cheerfully announced a quick update about something completely meaningless. The only thing that registered in Mike's foggy brain was her chipper "This is the Channel Seven eight o'clock news flash."

Eight o'clock? No way. It has to be almost midnight. I can't keep my eyes open. Suddenly Mike's body jerked, and he struggled to prop himself upright. He drew in a breath, then sucked in another in a horrified gasp.

"Gas!" That was what that cloying smell was— the stove was on!

"Wakefield!" Mike yelled, pushing against the

couch, trying to lever himself into a sitting position. He hadn't heard Steven leave, but maybe Mike had drifted off for a moment. Steven wouldn't have tried to . . . Mike shook his head, trying to clear it. He knew Steven hated him, hated him for what he'd done to Jessica, hated him for his own reasons. But he wouldn't have tried to kill him, would he? Finish the job the gun had started?

Feeling panicky, Mike pushed himself against the back of the couch. Oddly, the air was a tiny bit clearer up there than it had been when he was lying down. He shook his head again, remembering the horror of the shooting. No, Steven wasn't a killer.

"Wakefield!" he yelled again, reaching for the phone. No dial tone. *Dammit—when was that bill due?* Slamming down the phone, Mike tried to pull himself to his wheelchair. He thought he heard a muffled moan from the kitchen, but it was so low and faint he couldn't be sure. He managed to scoot clumsily to the end of the couch and grabbed for the arm of his wheelchair. Pulling it to him, he tried to shift his heavy, useless body into it, the way he vaguely remembered their showing him in physical therapy. Now, he thought grimly, he wished he'd paid more attention.

"Arrgh—ow! Damn!" The wheels spun out from under him, and Mike fell hard to the floor beside the couch. Wobbling crazily, the shiny chrome wheelchair skittered about five feet away.

8

Five impossible feet. Instantly Mike's head felt foggy again: The gas had sunk down to the floor, and was much thicker down there. *If I could walk I'd be OK,* Mike thought bitterly. But if he could walk, he wouldn't be in this mess in the first place. Setting his jaw, Mike began to pull himself along the dirty linoleum floor, and collapsed within a minute, breathing heavily. The gas was too strong down here. The floor seemed invitingly cool. *I have to rest a minute.*

Thoughts whirlpooled in his groggy brain: *Jessica, I love you. I'm sorry about what happened.* Now he would never see her again—unless he could somehow save himself, and Steven. Mike's teeth clenched with anger. *This is the tragedy. You're too weak and useless to help.*

Weak and useless. He would never get used to it. He was crippled! He couldn't even take care of himself. Steven was in the kitchen, probably unconscious, and his own strength was fading fast. They were going to die. There was nothing Mike could do. Balefully he glared at the wheelchair across the room.

I have to do something, he told himself. *I can't just give up.*

Using his superior upper-body strength, Mike put his palms flat on the floor and pressed himself upright, grasping for the back of the couch. He put his knees next to the couch and tried to balance his body weight on top of them. Once up, his knees gave out, and he almost collapsed again.

9

Face it, you're useless, a voice said. He snarled as he recalled the doctor's words: "You'll most likely never walk again. Maybe you'll feel tingles, or phantom pains in your legs. But you'll never walk again."

Then Mike heard a low moan from the kitchen: Steven.

Feeling an intense rage, Mike pounded on the couch. He swept the lamp off the end table, and it smashed against the wall into fragments of glass and metal.

"I won't let you win," he muttered through gritted teeth, unsure of whom he was defying. Maybe fate. Maybe life. "I can do it. I know I can do it. Get up, McAllery, you wimp. Get up!"

A cold sheen of sweat broke out on his forehead. Feeling as though his shoulder muscles were about to rip in two, he hauled himself up against the couch, clutching the upholstery so hard his knuckles turned white. But it was too much effort, and too much pain. The gas filled his nostrils, his mouth, his head, and he felt sick and dizzy. A drop of sweat rolled down into his eye and burned. He let go.

Steven's life was passing before his eyes. He saw his younger twin sisters, Elizabeth and Jessica, being brought home for the first time, in a white-wicker bassinet made especially for twins.

Then he was a little kid running across a field, an oversize helmet juggling around his head, a ball practically half his size clasped in his pudgy arms. His toddler sisters clapped their little palms together in approval.

Then he was older, and the field had turned into a court. He was jostled left and right. The squeaking sound of sneakers and the slap, slap, slap of a basketball filled the gym. He was surrounded by familiar faces, friends, teachers. He was a junior in high school; the twins were freshmen. He looked into the crowd and found his parents and his sister Elizabeth waving from the stands. And then Jessica, leaping up and down on the sideline with the cheerleaders, shouting his name.

His mind left the high-school gym, and he found himself at college, where he had met Billie, the most interesting and intelligent woman he'd ever known. . . . He remembered carrying her across the threshold of their apartment together, when they'd first decided to live together. It had been only one floor above this creep, this motorcycle-riding greaseball Mike McAllery. Then Mike's handsome, sneering face filled his vision. He was kissing Jessica in the garage. . . . Steven lunged for him.

"Jessica!" he cried.

He heard Mike's roar. "Where's my baby? Where is she? Jessica!"

"She's not yours!"

Jessica was cowering in the corner of Steven and Billie's apartment. Mike burst through the door with a gun, staggeringly drunk.

11

He felt the cool metal in his hand as he and Mike struggled for control. Mike shoved. Steven lost his balance. They went down together, the gun between them . . . down . . . down. Bang!

I'm dying, he thought.

He felt death overtaking him, stroking him like a cool, soothing breeze.

Not so bad. No pain. Peace. Warm. Seductive, like a beautiful day . . . I'm sorry, Billie, he thought. *Did I ever tell you? I love you.*

Chapter Two

"Hmm," Elizabeth murmured as she and Tom pulled apart. She was hardly conscious of the glaring fluorescent lights of the library, the scarred wooden carrels where they sat, the squeak of chairs around them. All she knew was the warmth and strength of Tom's arms, the fire of his kisses, the depth of yearning in his eyes.

"This is scary," Elizabeth whispered, putting one hand to her flushed cheek.

"Too much," Tom agreed unsteadily.

"Annoying," said a third voice from above them.

Startled, Elizabeth and Tom jumped, then looked up at the dark figure blocking the overhead light. The librarian, Mrs. Owensby, was standing over them, her hands on her hips, her mouth etched in a frown.

"Uh-oh," Tom said.

Mrs. Owensby shook her finger at them, looking fierce. "This is the fourth time this week I've

13

received complaints about you two."

Leaning back, Elizabeth poked her head around the carrel she and Tom were sharing. Up and down the row, faces she knew and faces she didn't—annoyed faces—were staring back at her. Her face flushed a deep, embarrassed pink.

"If I hear about you two engaging in inappropriate behavior in here just one more time," Mrs. Owensby said, "I am going to ask the dean to bar you from this library."

"Yes, Mrs. Owensby," Tom said quickly. "We understand."

"We're so sorry," Elizabeth muttered, looking at the floor.

When the librarian left, Elizabeth turned to Tom, her eyes wide. "I have never been so mortified in my entire life!" she said in a low tone, only half joking. "Good grief, you've got me acting like . . . like . . . well, like Jessica." Elizabeth's identical twin sister was famous for being anything but identical to Elizabeth in her behavior.

"I'm sure Mrs. Owensby was just trying to scare us," Tom said soothingly.

"Well, it worked!" Elizabeth said, lowering her voice further and glancing around. "The worst part is that she's right. We shouldn't be making out in the library." She shook her head wearily. "For some reason when I'm with you, all boundaries of common sense just fly out the window."

Tom grinned. "That's good news. But you're right. We shouldn't be doing this in a library."

Elizabeth nodded. "That's right. We should—"

"Go back to my room," Tom whispered, squeezing her thigh with his warm hand. "Then no one will complain."

"Tom!" Elizabeth blushed again. "I hate to say this, but I think maybe that until finals are over . . . we should take a break from each other. I'm going to flunk, otherwise." Looking over at Tom, she saw his handsome face creased in a dark frown. "Please don't be mad."

"I'm not mad," Tom said. "I'm just . . . sad at the thought of not spending every minute with you."

"But look," Elizabeth said cajolingly. "Look what we have to look forward to. In just another week we'll be going home for Christmas at my house—together. My parents have been dying to see you again; you really won them over on Parents' Weekend."

Tom grunted. "I don't know about that. What if they don't approve of me—of us—when they get to know me better? What if they don't think I'm good enough? You know: orphan, ex-jock, good-for-nothing *weirdo*." His voice ended with a note of despair.

"Oh, Tom, please. You're a famous journalist, a newsmaker. And, I might add, a hero who saved my life and blew the lid off the entire secret society single-handedly."

"Yeah. Me and twenty well-armed policemen."

"And another thing," Elizabeth went on, ignoring him, "you're gorgeous—but don't let that go to your head." Elizabeth kissed him lightly on the chin. "Besides, there's something important we're going to do when we go home. Look." She tugged the envelope-bookmark out of her textbook and dropped it into Tom's lap.

Tom opened the envelope and slid out an invitation card. His smile disappeared as he read it.

DEAR ALUM OF SWEET VALLEY HIGH
WE ARE PLEASED TO INVITE YOU AND A GUEST TO
YOUR GRADUATING CLASS'S FIRST REUNION
DECEMBER 26TH
SWEET VALLEY HIGH GYMNASIUM

Elizabeth leaned over and underlined with her pen the words "you and a guest." "We're going to my high-school reunion! It'll be so great!" She smiled at him excitedly.

"But . . . I . . . I . . ." Tom stumbled over his words.

"But first," Elizabeth said, solemn again, "we have to take our finals. And somehow pass." Putting her face close to his, she said softly, "I can't study when I'm with you, and I *have* to study. So . . ." She paused and put a hand on Tom's leg, locking her eyes with his. "Once we leave this library," she said earnestly, "we can't see each other until finals are over. That's only a week away. OK? Agreed?"

Tom frowned, and he sagged a little in his chair. "What about meals?" he said finally.

16

Elizabeth shrugged. "I don't know, Tom," she said reluctantly. "If I meet you for breakfast at nine in the morning, we'd still be there, making out, at noon. I think maybe we just have to go cold turkey. Just for a week. And then we'll go home, and have Christmas together, and go to the reunion . . ."

Tom frowned again, and for a moment Elizabeth wondered whether he was bummed about the reunion. She hoped not, because it was important to her that he be there. What better place to share her past with him than at the reunion, when it would all be there in one big room?

But that was silly, Elizabeth realized. She knew Tom was excited about the reunion. He was just unhappy that they weren't going to see each other until after exams. He looked so sad, it was all Elizabeth could do not to take him in her arms and comfort him. But they had to do this. They had to pass their finals, and the only way to pass their finals was to study, and there was only one way to study: *apart*.

"OK, so I'll take the library," Elizabeth said with forced brightness. "You hate study carrels, anyway. Maybe you can go to the TV station, right? You'll get a lot more work done there." She paused and bent down, trying to see his face. "Tom? It won't be so bad. You'll see. It'll be over before you know it."

"All right," Tom said finally, his voice defeated. "We'll study apart. But I have one last request."

Elizabeth waited patiently.

"I'll go now without a struggle on one condition: You have breakfast with me tomorrow. Please? It'll be our last breakfast until Christmas, and it'll help me go cold turkey if I know I'll see you tomorrow morning." His pleading eyes looked into hers.

Elizabeth felt herself relenting. What harm could one breakfast do? "OK. I'll meet you on the quad tomorrow at nine o'clock. Now go—let me get in at least one hour of real studying tonight."

"Deal."

"No!" Lila screamed. She sat up in bed, her long dark hair tangled around her face and throat. Her heart was pounding and she was gasping for air. Wildly, she looked at the clock on her night table. It was only eleven o'clock. Slowly she forced her breathing to calm, and she brushed her hair away from her face. The sheets were damp with sweat and wrapped confiningly around her legs, as though she'd been thrashing. But it was OK now. She was in her own bed, in her own room, at her parents' house in Sweet Valley.

"God," she muttered, taking a sip of water from the glass on her night table. "So much for turning in early to get a good night's sleep." She must have been asleep only half an hour, but it had been plenty of time for a horrific nightmare.

She got out of bed, went to the bathroom, and splashed cold water on her face. Her eyes were large and frightened looking, and her face was pale. Taking a deep breath, she went back to her room and straightened the covers. She wondered if she should fix herself a glass of warm milk. Of course not. Warm milk was repulsive.

Lila climbed back into bed and arranged the covers neatly over herself. It wasn't the first nightmare she'd had—far from it. She had been present at the death of her husband, Tisiano di Mondicci. He'd been racing his boat far too fast on the Italian Riviera. She'd been sunning herself on the beach, waiting for him to finish and come get her so they could go do something fun together. Right in front of her eyes she'd seen his boat flip, skid along the water upside down, then explode in a huge fireball. Right in front of her eyes.

Ever since then she'd replayed the scene in her mind again and again in nightmares. Sometimes the dreams were worse than others—sometimes she dreamed she actually saw and held his mangled body, burned beyond recognition.

Sliding down under the covers, she frowned. This dream just now had been different. In it she'd had the same familiar nightmare about Tisiano. She'd seen his boat explode again. Every detail was etched on her memory. But at the end she'd been in a small plane. She'd been heading home to Sweet Valley after Tisiano's funeral. In this dream the little plane was shaking. Her teeth were rattling. Strong winds were tossing the plane back and forth, and as she watched in horror, a bank of mountains came up to meet them much too fast. Then Lila had been outside the plane, watching it as though from a distance. The little plane had been tossed against the side of the mountain and had instantly exploded. A fireball had formed, just like the one from Tisiano's boat. In the dream Lila knew that she'd been on the plane, and that she was dead now. That was when she'd woken up screaming.

But what did it mean? In Italy, for lack of anything better to do, she'd taken flying lessons. Amazingly enough, it had turned out to be the one thing she was good at, besides shopping. She'd even gotten her private pilot's license. Since coming back to Sweet Valley, she hadn't taken a plane up by herself. Was the dream a premonition of some kind? Did it mean that she was going to kill herself if she continued flying? Or did it only mean that she was scared of that happening?

Maybe Bruce had caused the whole nightmare, she thought with a small touch of anger. Bruce Patman had been the bane of her existence all through high school, and running into him on the Sweet Valley U campus hadn't improved her life any. One year older than she, he'd always lorded it over Lila that Patman money was old money, and Fowler money was new money. As if it were something to be ashamed of, Lila thought with a sneer.

Anyway, once she was on campus at SVU, seeing all her friends again, preparing to audit courses, choosing to pledge the Theta sorority, she'd run into him again. He hadn't gotten any better with age. Sure, he was still good-looking, if you liked tall, well-built guys with deep-blue eyes. But he was still just as obnoxious as ever. When he'd heard that Lila had her pilot's license, he'd said he had his, too, and he'd challenged her to show him what she knew. What was worse, he'd recently inherited a billion dollars or something, and it had gone right to his head, which he could hardly fit through a door in the first place. Now he had his own plane, and he kept buzzing the SVU dorms in a completely aggravating way. The dean had actually called him into his office and ordered him to stop.

That must be it, Lila thought in the darkness of her room. She didn't know for sure, but she suspected it had just been Bruce's boasting invading her dreams, giving her nightmares. But now what mattered was that she was exhausted and had to get some sleep. Forcing herself not to feel afraid, she snuggled down again and closed her eyes.

I will not dream about Tisiano. I will not dream about Tisiano. I will not dream about Tisiano.

Chapter
Three

Mike expected to fall backward, to crash again on the floor. But he didn't. Inexplicably, he remained on his knees, balanced. He looked down unbelievingly. The floor felt hard and painful against his knees—but, of course, that was impossible, he reminded himself. He had no feeling there.

Then, after hesitating a moment, Mike turned a bit and let himself fall forward on his hands. Instead of his knees splaying out uselessly beneath him, they stayed locked in place. He was on all fours for the first time since the gunshot.

A bead of sweat trickled down the side of his face. The smell of gas made him feel nauseated, and he tried to hold his breath. Slowly, carefully, he put his hands on the floor a bit ahead of him, then pulled his knees in. Again, he put his hands in front, then pulled his knees forward. He had moved almost a yard.

A pathetic sense of joy flooded him, making

him feel almost as weak and dizzy as the escaping gas. He was mobile—on his own. He was actually moving without help. It was exhilarating. A burst of adrenaline raced through him, filling him with new energy and increasing his sense of urgency. *Hang on, Wakefield. Help is on the way.*

Hands, then knees. Hands, then knees. With practice he became almost quick at it, almost natural. The knees of his black jeans were caked with dirt from the floor, and his palms felt filthy and gritty. His T-shirt was damp with sweat, and his dark hair hung limply in his eyes. But he was almost at the kitchen door.

The stench of gas was much thicker there, and Mike gagged, pressing one hand against his mouth. He almost toppled over, losing his balance, but caught himself.

Then he was at the door. Steven was lying motionless on the linoleum, and Mike slid his way to him as fast as he could. Practically overcome, holding his breath, Mike bent down and gripped Steven by the shirt. Steven's eyes were closed, his face gray. Was he dead? Gulping, Mike looked for the motion of breathing and saw none. Clumsily his fingers pawed at Steven's neck, searching for a pulse. There! It was faint, and unsteady, but it was there. *Thank God.*

But what now? The gas was overwhelming—he was about to succumb to it himself. Brushing his damp hair out of his eyes, he peered up at the front door. It looked about five miles away. Mike tentatively tried to pull Steven, then push him. But Steven weighed more than Mike, and it felt absolutely hopeless.

A sob choked Mike's throat. He could move again; he had this incredible feeling of independence, of strength, and now it was all for nothing. The gas burned his eyes and his throat. What to do, what to do?

Then he had an idea. Gently he let Steven's head down to the floor again and made his way over to the kitchen door. The door was propped open with a cast-iron Scottie dog that Jessica had found at some flea market. Mike thought the dog was hideous, but now it might actually be useful.

He pulled the doorstop toward him, and the kitchen door swung closed, trapping Mike with Steven in the gas-filled room.

This better work. With all his might, feeling his arm muscles trembling with the exertion, Mike dragged himself over to the floor under the kitchen window. Then he sat up, braced himself, and lifted the doorstop in both hands. A sudden wave of dizziness and nausea overwhelmed him, but with a mighty heave, he hurled the doorstop toward the window.

The heavy weight smashed through the glass and tumbled two stories to the ground. Numbly, Mike hoped no one had been standing below. But the window was broken, and fresh, sweet waves of clean night air billowed into the room. Almost instantly Mike's head felt clearer. Taking in huge gulps of fresh air, he slid on his hands and knees over to the stove. By bracing his knees under him he was able to rear up and snap off the burner with a flick of his wrist. The insidious hiss of escaping gas ceased. *Thank God.*

His knees hurt, he realized with surprise. Hurt from supporting his weight against the floor. He actually thought he could feel his knees. The doctors were wrong! *Don't worry about it now,* Mike commanded himself. *Keep moving!*

"Steven! Steven!"

He slapped Steven in the face, but Steven's eyes stayed shut. His skin was ash-gray, his lips blue. Agonized, Mike felt again for a pulse, but this time felt nothing. All his efforts had been in vain. Steven was dead! "It was Mike's fault," Mike heard Jessica say in his mind. "He was too weak. He couldn't do it. He couldn't save my brother."

"Steven!" Mike yelled again.

Someone pounded on his front door. "What's going on in there? Do you know what time it is? Who broke the window?" an older man's voice cried.

"Call an ambulance!" Mike yelled as loud as he could. He could hear other people gathering around the door.

But there was no time to wait for help. This too would be up to him. He fell on his hands and knees, pried open Steven's mouth, tilted back his head, pinched his nose shut, and pressed his own mouth to Steven's. He breathed and counted.

One . . . two . . . three. Breathed again. Counted one . . . two . . . three. And breathed again . . .

In the early-morning sun, Jessica Wakefield walked slowly across the campus quad, holding her books to her chest like a shield. Her eyes squinted in the harsh brightness of sunlight. It was almost nine o'clock, an hour Jessica didn't remember being awake at in months. The day was bright and welcoming, and the sky over the SVU campus was a pale, cloudless blue. A soft, cool wind carried the damp scent of wet grass. It was a southern-California morning that could be brimming full of possibility and excitement.

But it wasn't. In Jessica's fist was her invitation to the high-school reunion. Her blue-green eyes were stormy as she plodded across the quad.

How can I show my face there after everything that's happened? The very thought was totally depressing.

Moving in with Mike McAllery, eloping for a quickie wedding in Las Vegas . . . and then Steven accidentally shooting him, paralyzing Mike from the waist down—it was too much to believe, like a bad soap opera. She herself wouldn't believe it if it hadn't all happened to her.

Everyone'll have some gorgeous hunk or some stunning model type on their arm, she thought with a sigh. *They'll come waltzing in looking ten times better than me. Who'll I have? Who'll I be? I can't possibly show my face. I'd be mortified.*

As Jessica neared a trash can, she crumpled the invitation and dropped it in.

"Well, that's settled," she said aloud. But she still had the rest of the day to face. For the last two days she'd been a nervous wreck—ever since her best friend and former roommate, Isabella Ricci, had suggested she come over to the Theta house that morning for a cram session.

"And who knows?" Isabella had said with a wink. "Maybe we'll find some way to convince the Thetas to renew their pledge offer to you."

The pledge I've wanted since the day I got here four months ago, Jessica reminded herself. It had gone out the window when Jessica had taken up with bad-news Mike McAllery.

Jessica looked left and right, hoping she wouldn't run into anyone she knew. It was a gorgeous morning, and not only was she awake now—at a time when only bird-watchers or nerds should be conscious—but she was alone. And carrying schoolbooks! This was as close to humility as she would get.

Suddenly Jessica stopped short and ducked behind a palm tree. Across the quad her twin sister, Elizabeth, was walking along a path with her new boyfriend, Tom Watts. Elizabeth and Tom were holding hands, but they both looked serious and a little sad. *Uh-oh. I hope there isn't trouble in paradise,* Jessica thought. She knew she'd get the whole story from Elizabeth later. *I'm surprised they get anywhere at all, since they can't take their eyes*

27

off of each other long enough to see where they're going. Jessica saw Elizabeth suddenly smile at Tom and nod at something he said. Then he bent down and pulled Elizabeth into a romantic embrace.

Boy, have times changed, she thought. The Wakefield twins *looked* identical—they were both five foot six and had matching blue-green eyes, long golden-blond hair, and dimples in their left cheeks—but that was where the resemblance ended. Inside, the twins couldn't have been more different. Elizabeth had always been the hardworking and dependable one, the one who read up on world events and sold "Save Our Planet" T-shirts for the Environmental Awareness Club, the one people went to for help or a sympathetic ear. Jessica had always been frivolous and wild, more interested in fun and boys than in good deeds, always on the prowl for the opportunity to have a good time. She was flirty, outrageous, and impulsive, and she liked it that way.

Or at least she had, until now. *Everything's different now*, she thought, peeking out from behind her tree. *Elizabeth is gaga in love, skipping all over campus as if she doesn't have a care in the world. And I'm about to spend a beautiful day over at the Theta house, begging to be allowed to cram with them—for a psych final, of all things! I can't believe the only romance in my life is what I see by spying on Elizabeth*. Talk about pathetic.

She watched as Elizabeth and Tom broke from their embrace and was surprised to see Tom walk

28

away alone while her twin turned around and headed to the library.

Jessica sighed and turned away. She felt as if she had just arrived at freshman orientation all over again—as if she didn't know anyone, didn't know where to go, didn't know what to do with herself.

Moments later Jessica wavered on her feet in front of Theta house. She had a pang of regret as she mentally compared the homey and luxurious Theta rooms with the anonymous cinder-block cave she shared with Elizabeth. The Thetas had been within her grasp, and she'd blown them off for Mike. Well, she'd learned her lesson, and she was back.

Walking up to the large, impressive front door, she raised her hand to knock. She knew all too well that her chances of renewing her pledge might be completely hopeless. For one thing, Theta vice-president Alison Quinn hated her guts. Jessica's hasty, disastrous marriage to Mike McAllery had gone a long way to destroying her reputation forever. And there was also the fact that Jessica had taken a job waitressing at a coffee house because she'd run out of money. Theta girls just didn't do that kind of thing. When Alison had shown up at the restaurant one night, only to see Jessica in her uniform struggling with a tray of food, Jessica had practically seen her pledge vaporize before her eyes.

Suddenly Jessica felt like a leper—damaged goods. *Why am I kidding myself? Who would want me now?* she thought despondently, turning to walk away. Then she stopped.

Hold on. What am I saying? I'm Jessica Wakefield. I was hot at Sweet Valley High, and I'll be hot here, too. Those Theta snobs don't have anything I don't have. I'm not only as good as any of those girls in there, I'm better. I have experience they never would have dreamed of—I've lived. I'm a woman now, and they're all still teenagers. They should all look up to me.

Jessica whirled, stalked up the stairs, and raised her hand.

But just as she was about to knock, the door opened a tiny bit. Isabella slid out through the crack.

"Hi, Isabella," Jessica said confidently. "Here I am."

"Shh," Isabella hissed. She looked worriedly over Jessica's shoulder. "Alison's not here right now, so the coast is clear. We've got to get everyone on your side before she gets back."

"What do you want me to do?" Jessica asked.

Isabella thoughtfully looked Jessica over.

Early this morning, as Jessica had blearily pawed through her closet, she'd automatically grabbed a body-hugging knit dress in a fine, deep blue. It was stylish and daring, and showed off her perfect size-six figure. But then she'd remembered she was trying to impress a bunch of *girls,* and Theta girls, at that. The last thing she wanted to do was make someone jealous.

So of course she'd had to go to Elizabeth's closet. A neat white blouse buttoned to the collar and a long navy-blue skirt filled the bill. Topped off with a tweedy jacket, she looked a little dowdy, a little prim. But it was just this side of being acceptably fashionable, especially with those two-tone oxfords and white socks. They wouldn't recognize her. Just the image she wanted to give. The new Jessica Wakefield.

"You look great, Jess," Isabella said. "I hope Elizabeth doesn't mind your borrowing her clothes." She searched the street again with her eyes, then grabbed Jessica's hand and pulled her inside. "Just be yourself—only a little less so, OK?"

Chapter
Four

_____

"Uhhh," Alexandra Rollins moaned, rolling over in her bed. Even without opening her eyes, she knew she was sick. She must have caught some awful stomach bug or eaten something bad. She felt like death.

Very, very slowly she pried her eyes open, wincing as the filtered light from the window started assaulting her senses. It was a new day, but she had no idea what time it was. Groaning quietly, she tried to prop herself up on her elbows.

Mistake. As soon as her head rose off her pillow, the room started to spin sickeningly. Whimpering, she quickly lay back down and closed her eyes, but it was too late. The world was spinning in uneven circles, and her bed felt like a hammock in some tiny storm-tossed sailboat.

I'm gonna barf. This realization was enough to shock Alexandra into throwing off the covers and lunging for the bathroom. Making it just in time, she pulled up the toilet seat, fell to her knees, and drove the porcelain bus for what seemed like at least half an hour.

Finally her stomach was totally empty, more than empty, cavernously empty. Almost weeping with revulsion and sickness, Alexandra sat on the cool tile of the bathroom floor until she felt as if she could stand up without fainting. Then she splashed cold water over her face at the sink and took a gulp of mouthwash. After swirling and spitting, she groped for her toothbrush and brushed her teeth for as long as she could. Then she used her mouthwash again.

Finally, after wetting a cold washcloth and draping it over the back of her neck, she ventured to look in the mirror. She actually felt much better—not so dizzy and nauseated anymore, and she knew she would feel even better after a nice hot shower. That's why the image in the mirror was such a total and revolting shock.

Oh, God. That can't be me. Alexandra stared at the face staring back at her. Her eyes were bloodshot and had dark circles around them. Her skin was pasty and dull, her nose red, and her hair was frightening. *I must really be sick,* she thought weakly. *I'd better go lie down.* She made her way back to her bed and sat there gingerly.

She squinted across the room at her roommate's bed. It was empty, the blankets drum-tight, the pillows fluffed. It looked as if it belonged to nobody, like a motel bed.

When is the last time Trina slept here? Alexandra wondered, feeling a tiny bit envious. Ever since her roommate had found a boyfriend, Alexandra had essentially been living in a single. Which wasn't the worst thing in the world, she admitted. Though at times, like now, she could have used a friendly voice and a helping hand.

Alexandra sighed, feeling very sorry for herself. Once again, in her mind's eye, she saw Mark Gathers's Ford Explorer turn the corner for the last time and head toward L.A. *I wonder if he made the Lakers,* she thought. *I wonder if they even gave him a tryout.* Alexandra had met Mark soon after the semester had started. They had become serious pretty fast, and Mark had been Alexandra's first lover. Then everything had fallen apart.

Last month Elizabeth Wakefield and Tom Watts had broken open the athletic-department recruitment scandal. Mark had been stripped of his eligibility and kicked off the basketball team. The very next day he had left SVU—and Alexandra—swearing that he could still make it as a basketball player. He meant in the NBA.

I wonder if he's thinking of me the way I'm thinking of him, Alexandra mused.

She looked at her reflection and sighed. "Not a chance," she said aloud. A cream-colored sheet of paper on her night table caught her eye. The Sweet Valley High reunion. Her heart sank one level deeper. She imagined herself walking through the doors of the Sweet Valley High gym on Mark's arm. All the guys were nodding with approval, and all the girls were silenced by envy. For the first time in her life she was popular, she was attractive, she was cool. Mark had been everything she'd wanted, the sort of guy who just by stepping into a room could wipe out Alexandra's old image: the nerdy, awkward *Enid* Rollins.

Now she saw herself walking into the gym alone. "Oh, hey, Enid," everyone would say, sounding bored.

Where was Alexandra? Where was her fresh start as someone new, someone exciting and different?

"The more things change," she groaned, "the more they stay the same." That did it. She definitely needed a hot shower. Back in the bathroom she gave another glance in the mirror, hoping against hope that her appearance had improved dramatically. It hadn't.

Suddenly Alexandra spotted something else in the mirror. She raised her chin to see it better. She started probing with her fingers. There. A little bruise on her neck. And another one. What the hell was that? She leaned closer to the mirror. They weren't red, they were purplish, like . . .

"Hickies?" she groaned. "But . . . how?"

Her eyes widened as it all started coming back to her, some memory of something . . . it felt like years ago—she could hardly picture it. Long ago and yet . . . *yesterday*. Last *night*. Slowly, dimly, she pieced things together in her mind like a jigsaw puzzle.

She was walking across the quad on the way to the library to study. Someone called out to her. Mark? No. He's in Los Angeles. No—Todd! Oh, my God!

Everything came back in a rush. Todd Wilkins! She remembered their conversation. They were both lonely, bored, overwhelmed with finals. A beautiful night, too nice to study. *Let's get a drink,* someone had said. Who'd said that? Why couldn't she remember?

But when I drink, I get so stupid!

Later Todd had stalked into her room without knocking, armed with a flask of Scotch. They'd talked about how badly Elizabeth was treating Todd—as if she didn't know him. Alexandra had brought up the idea of changing her name back to Enid. She winced as she remembered Todd's reaction: He'd patted the space next to him on her bed. "You're a lot sweeter and sexier than Enid was," he'd slurred, already drunk. She'd smiled back at him through her tears. He'd put his arms around her shoulders. She remembered what that felt like, his warm muscular body against hers, and for a minute it was as if they weren't just friends. It was as if that kiss he'd given her the week before had really meant something. They had been drunk then, too. She'd passed it off as a drunken mistake. But now she didn't know.

Feeling shocked, she staggered back into her room and sank down on her bed. "Oh, no," she moaned. "What did we do? Did Todd stay here? Did

36

we . . . ?" Horrified, she glanced down at herself.

Todd Wilkins? Elizabeth's ex-boyfriend? Todd Wilkins, who adored Elizabeth and vowed not to give up on her until the day he died?

OK, OK, calm down. *Think, Alex, think!* She shut her eyes and searched her mental files, but all she saw was fog and cobwebs. They had gotten drunk together. That much she knew. He'd kissed her. . . . She remembered lying back against her bed, his body pressed against hers. . . .

Alexandra's eyes blinked open. She glared at the bed, as if demanding it to fill in the blank. Quickly she leaned over, ignoring the insistent pounding of her head, and grabbed for the drawer in her night table. When she and Mark had been together, they'd usually stayed at his place. But sometimes, when they didn't want to bother crossing the campus, they'd crashed here. And just in case, she'd kept a packet of condoms—in the top drawer of her nightstand. But it was empty now.

Steven tried to smile but couldn't. His face hurt. In fact, his entire body hurt. He forced his eyes open but didn't recognize his surroundings. Looking around in confusion, he realized he was in a hospital room. A patterned curtain was drawn around his bed. Then his eyes fell on Mike, who was sitting in a wheelchair a few feet away, watching him.

"What happened?" he croaked. "Where am I? What time is it?"

"You're in the hospital," Mike said. "The hospital bed and the machines should be a clue," he added with mild sarcasm. "It's morning. You've been here all night."

All of a sudden it all came back to him: the thick, sickly-sweet smell of gas in Mike's apartment . . . reaching for the stove, not making it . . . the dizziness, falling, then the relief of blackness and unconsciousness.

"Mike," he whispered hoarsely, trying to raise his head. "The stove, the gas—"

"Yeah. It took me a while to figure out that the reason you were still in the kitchen wasn't because you'd decided to rearrange all my shelves." Mike gave a lopsided grin.

"How did I—how did you?" Steven's head ached, and the light hurt his eyes, but he needed some answers.

"I threw a doorstop through the window," Mike said casually. "Let in some fresh air. Then a neighbor called an ambulance."

"You got into your wheelchair by yourself?"

Mike looked away, wheeling himself back and forth in little repetitive motions. "Not exactly. I messed up with the wheelchair—couldn't get to it. I sort of slithered to the kitchen." Again his bright, hard smile.

"So you saved my life," Steven said.

"Yeah, well, an eye for an eye," Mike answered flippantly.

"What do you mean?" Steven asked, feeling as

if a trap were lying in wait for him somewhere.

"The shooting changed my life," Mike said simply.

Steven closed his eyes and turned his head away. *I know it did,* he thought painfully. *You'll be spending the rest of it in a wheelchair, thanks to me.*

"No," Mike said, seeming to read the expression crossing Steven's face. "I mean I was headed for trouble before the accident. I know what I was doing to Jessica was wrong. I was being a total jerk. In another couple of months I probably would have ended up wrecking my bike or drinking myself to death." His voice was gruff, and he didn't look at Steven. "In a way the accident made me take a good look at myself. And I didn't like what I saw."

Steven looked across the metal frame of his hospital bed. Was Mike telling the truth? Had he really changed for the better? "So what happens now?" he said out loud.

"Well." Mike shrugged. "Last night I realized something weird. I was trying to get to you—I thought we were both going to die. My damn phone wasn't working, and I knew it was up to me either to save us both or die with you." He smirked. "The thought of how mad Jessica would be at me if I let anything happen to you gave me new strength."

Steven tried to muffle his snort of laughter.

"I mean, she'd haul me out of my grave and kill me again, you know?" Mike said. "So I just tried anything I could to get to you. And I found out that I have some feeling in my legs."

"What!" Steven stared at Mike. "The doctors said you never would."

"I know," Mike said smugly. "But I do. Not only that, but all morning I've been wiggling my toes. Look."

Steven craned his head over the side of his bed and looked down at Mike's cowboy boots. Sure enough, the tip of one boot was moving ever so slightly.

"Mike! That's fantastic!" he cried.

"Yeah. So I'm working on it. I'm going to start doing my rehab exercises again. Who knows? Maybe I'll get out of this damn chair once and for all."

"I really hope so, Mike," Steven said sincerely. True, this was the guy who had broken Jessica's heart and practically ruined her life. True, Steven had wished him dead on more than one occasion. But now, after working with Mike so closely for several weeks, he had come to see more than the hell-raiser, more than the jerk Mike presented to the world. Now when he looked at Mike, he saw someone with potential, someone who needed a break. Someone who deserved to live, and to walk again.

"Listen, you let me know if I can help, OK?" Steven said. Then he frowned. "But if you think I'm doing your stinky laundry again . . ."

The small hospital room filled with their laughter.

*   *   *

"Sigmund Freud and Carl Jung—discuss amongst yourselves," Isabella said, waving her hands in little circles, imitating her favorite comedian from *Saturday Night Live*.

A groan passed through the room of Theta sorority sisters.

"I say we just drink more coffee," Lila Fowler said. "This is *so* dull."

Isabella rolled her eyes. "Gee, Lila, thanks for your moral support," she said. "I'm so glad you came to study with us. But remember, *we* have to take this exam."

"Oh, why bother?" Denise Waters moaned, brushing her brown hair from her shoulders. "There's too much to learn. And it's too hard. I like Lila's idea. I'll just go whip us up some iced cappuccino. . . ."

"I know who Freud was," Jessica blurted. "And Jung."

"Come on, Jess," Denise said. "Stop kidding around. We have more important things to do. Like make coffee." She stood to head into the kitchen.

"No, listen, guys. Really. Sigmund Freud, born 1856, died 1939, Austrian, was the father of psychoanalysis," Jessica recited from memory.

"Oooh, go, girl," Lila said, pretending to be impressed.

Jessica ignored her and went on. "Carl Jung, born 1875, Swiss, was another psychologist who agreed with many of Freud's methods. But eventually they split over a patient, a woman, who some say they both secretly fell in love with. Personally, I think that Freud and Jung were the two most influential minds of the twentieth century. Almost all of the modern symbols and metaphors we use today came from one or the other of them. Not to mention the entire school of dream interpretation to unlock the deep subconscious." She shifted in her chair and smoothed her skirt self-consciously.

No one in the room moved. It was completely silent. Seven pairs of wide eyes were locked on Jessica.

Outwardly, Jessica was the picture of calm, but inwardly, she was grinning. She couldn't believe she knew this stuff, but she did. And she was wowing the Thetas. Everything was going perfectly according to plan. She could practically read their minds. *Jessica Wakefield,* they were thinking. *What a woman.*

"Should I go on?" she asked innocently.

"Sure, Jess. Go ahead," Isabella said, giving Jessica a thumbs-up sign. Looking smug, Isabella leaned back against the chintz couch and raised her pen to take notes.

Jessica sat up straight and began to list Freud's and Jung's major accomplishments. After a few minutes other Theta sisters pulled out their notebooks and begin taking notes also.

When Jessica stopped, Isabella led the girls in a round of applause.

"Well, Jess," Lila said, her dark eyebrows lifting with surprise. "I never thought I'd see the day, but I have to hand it to you. It isn't an act. You really have changed while I was gone."

Jessica couldn't help preening a bit. She and Lila had been best friends practically since kindergarten: to surprise Lila took some doing. Now that her friend was back, Jessica wondered if Lila would surprise her, too. When Lila had married Tisiano, everyone had been jealous, but no one more so than Jessica. It didn't seem fair—after all, Lila already had everything. Incredibly rich, sophisticated, a gorgeous brunette with killer eyes and long dark hair, her glamorous life only became more glamorous.

When Lila had married Tisiano de Mondicci, she'd become a European socialite and a fabulously wealthy countess. And all her friends in Sweet Valley had become just—college freshmen. Every now and then, while she'd been was toiling over her books, going through one ordeal after another with Mike, dealing with her money woes, Jessica had thought of her friend Lila, sunning herself on the Italian Riviera. She'd figured that probably the only things Lila was toiling through were cocktail parties, what dress to wear, whether to hire another maid; that the only work she ever did was on her Italian, or her perfect tan.

But a couple of weeks ago everything had changed. Tisiano had died, and Lila had returned to southern California to start her life all over again as—what else? A college freshman at SVU.

"That's right, Jess," Isabella said, interrupting her thoughts about Lila. "You've really put your nose to the grindstone. I, for one, am impressed." She winked at Jessica from across the room.

"Me too," Denise chimed in.

"Well, I'm not," a voice said.

Everyone looked up. Alison Quinn stood in the doorway, her chilly gray eyes flashing with anger. With a flick of her head she tossed her perfect golden hair over her shoulder.

"What's *she* doing here?" she asked, nodding in Jessica's direction. "I thought we agreed no guests during finals week."

Denise rolled her eyes. "Come on, Alison," she said. "Get a life. We're studying."

Alison turned red with anger and looked ready to charge at Denise.

I really like that girl, Jessica thought.

Isabella stepped forward to intercept Alison. "We did agree, Alison, but Jess—"

"No guests during finals week," Alison reminded them coldly.

"What about me?" Lila pointed out. "You said it was all right for *me* to hang out here—"

"No *unwanted* guests," Alison amended. Her eyes flashed, passing through Jessica as if she were invisible, as if she weren't standing right in front of her. "We all agreed."

Alison stalked out, and Jessica saw her hopes of repledging the Thetas stalk out with her.

44

"Sorry, Jess," Denise said, looking sincere. "If it was up to me, you could move in today."

"Thanks," Jessica said with a sad smile.

Lila offered her another muffin to cheer her up, but Jessica just shook her head and looked up at her old friend. Lila was being allowed to stay—Jessica wasn't. But seeing Lila's sympathetic eyes reminded her of what true heartbreak was all about. Sure, Jessica had had her problems, and right now she was totally bummed about that witch Alison. But Lila's husband had been killed. Lila's life had literally been turned upside down. She couldn't begrudge Lila being allowed to stay with the Thetas.

"Do you want me to walk you home?" Lila asked.

"No, stay and study," Jessica said, feeling a little better. Without warning she gave her friend a hug.

"What was that for?" Lila exclaimed.

"Do I need a reason?" Jessica called behind her as she walked out the door. "Why does everyone look so sad? It's a beautiful day! Now I'll just have to go out and enjoy it." Waving cheerfully, she let herself out the door with a jaunty step.

But as she stepped out into the bright morning sunlight, leaving the Theta house and her friends behind her, she couldn't deny that how she really felt was disappointed and lonely.

Chapter Five

Elizabeth sat at her desk in her dorm room, her face cradled in her hands. After having breakfast with Tom, she'd tried to study in the library, but she hadn't been able to get any work done. There were too many other people around, even if they were being quiet, and too many other books to look at. There were too many distractions. Elizabeth had decided to go back to her room and study.

At the moment she was surrounded by her newest favorite subject, the literature of African-American writers. She was supposed to be skimming through her notes on Zora Neal Hurston's *Their Eyes Were Watching God*. She'd already read it twice and had loved it. Hurston's writing was like music, and usually Elizabeth could get lost in its rhythms in minutes. But now her eyes were skating right over the text. Instead of seeing the words on the page, she saw only a series of black smudges. She just couldn't get Tom out of her mind. She could still see him, feel him, taste him on her lips. . . .

She was groggy, lovesick, and unmotivated to do work for the first time in her life. She had been a diligent student her whole life; she didn't know how to be a loafer whose mind drifted everywhere but where it should be.

"Is this what it's like to be Jessica?" she muttered. "It's exhausting."

For the tenth time in the last hour, Elizabeth threw a longing glance toward her bed. After staying late last night with Tom, saying good-bye, and then getting up so early today to have their last breakfast together, she felt as if she were about to drop. She was so tired . . . maybe she could take just a little nap . . . just ten minutes of lying under the cozy covers, staring at the ceiling, daydreaming about . . .

Suddenly she imagined the expression on her parents' faces when she handed them her grades.

No! she commanded herself. *I can't give in.*

Elizabeth stood up, her eyes sweeping around the small dorm room. One half was a mess, of course. Jessica's clothes bulged from the closet and spilled from the drawers of her bureau. The blankets on her bed were rumpled. Mismatched shoes were scattered across the floor. Notebooks and pens peeked out from beneath the bed. *Well, if I really want to procrastinate,* Elizabeth thought, *I could try cleaning up Jessica's side of the room. That would kill about ten or eleven hours.*

But Elizabeth knew it wasn't Jessica's mess that was keeping her from work. It was Tom. She had to find a way to stop thinking about him. Elizabeth moved around the room with a mission, putting all traces of Tom out of sight. All of Tom's pictures and letters to her were put in a drawer. A shirt of his was hanging on her doorknob, and she tossed it into her laundry bag. Then she frowned, sniffing the air. She really could still smell him. It was *her* shirt, she finally realized. Of course, there had been all that hugging and kissing this morning at breakfast. Elizabeth added her shirt to his in the laundry basket and put on a clean one. Then she went back to work, elbows on desk, face in hands.

Concentrate!

After about a minute her eyes had drifted from her notes to the window, through the trees, toward Tom's dorm.

With a resigned moan she got up and threw herself on the bed. She had to get him out of her mind. She had to get away from this bed, from this room.

She sat bolt upright, struck by an idea. Reaching for the phone, she dialed her friend Nina Harper's number. Nina knew those writers backward and forward. Although she was a chem major, she was incredibly well read. Nina had a heart of gold and was maybe the most loyal friend Elizabeth had. She was also a totally anal-retentive student. Ruthless. Unforgiving. Disciplined.

Ruthless. Unforgiving. Disciplined, Elizabeth thought happily. *That's just what I need.*

"Nina?" Elizabeth said into the receiver. "I'm in big trouble. You have to help me. I'm coming right over."

Todd Wilkins opened one eye, then the other, then closed both, shielding them from the light pouring in through the window blinds. He groaned. He was wrecked.

"What did I *do* last night?" he muttered. "I must have really gotten faced."

Where had he been last night? His mouth felt dry, his tongue was thick and cottony. As bad as he felt, he could smell the alcohol on his breath, his sweat. All he wanted right now was an ice-cold ginger ale with all the bubbles out of it. He wanted a wet washcloth. He wanted a bucket.

Uncomfortably, he squirmed around on his bed. It was lumpy, and his belt buckle was digging into his back. He forced his eyes open farther and tried to sit up. Frowning, he looked at the scene before him.

He was lying on top of his covers. Looked like he never actually made it *into* bed last night. He was wearing a T-shirt, his jeans, and one sock. Looked like he never actually got undressed last night. The T-shirt was inside out. Carefully, trying not to disturb the racket going on inside his brain, he peeled off the shirt. It smelled like perfume. He frowned at it. He didn't recognize it. It wasn't even his shirt. Whose was it?

Just then Todd decided it would be a good idea to go splash water on his face. He stood up slowly and staggered toward the bathroom. Hanging over the sink, he cupped his hands and slurped up as much water as he could hold. Then he pawed at the medicine cabinet until a bottle of aspirin fell into the sink. He took four.

Squinting at himself in the mirror, he saw a not too pretty picture staring back at him. He needed a shower and a shave, and his eyes were bloodshot. His back felt irritated, and it stung a little bit. Maybe he'd scraped himself on his belt buckle. Twisting his body around, he tried to see the place in the mirror. His eyes narrowed. What had happened to him? There were several small pink scratches running across his back. Had he hurt himself somehow last night? Was that why someone had given him a new shirt?

As he tried to piece together the picture of the previous evening, he felt a dim sense of dread overtake him and settle in his stomach.

The scene was gradually coming back to him: Drinking by himself. Seeing Alexandra. Asking her if she wanted a drink. Then, later, in the comforting, dim light of her room, she was crying for some reason, God knew why. He wanted to soothe her. She had been warm and soft. Her mouth had opened under his, they had fallen back onto her bed . . . and now here he was, wearing her shirt and with scratches on his back!

"Oh, man!" Todd cried, making his way back to his bed and falling onto it. He buried his head in his pillow. "What have I done? What an idiot!" He couldn't have slept with Alexandra—*Enid* Rollins! Elizabeth's ex–best friend! He rolled over against the wall, appalled. "How did life get so bad so quickly?" he asked the wall.

First he'd dumped his longtime girlfriend, Elizabeth, because she wouldn't sleep with him. Almost immediately he'd taken up with slinky but basically uninteresting Lauren Hill, only to find out during the sports-recruiting investigation how unsupportive and selfish she really was. It had hit him in his gut that he was still in love with Elizabeth. Then he was suspended from the basketball team for one year because he'd accepted illegal preferential treatment from the athletic department. Then, right when he needed her most, Elizabeth had fallen in love with that journalist geek Tom Watts. She was probably sleeping with him, he thought bitterly.

Now, just to top it all off and make his freshman year absolutely the worst year of his entire life, he had probably—he wasn't positive—but he may have just done it with Elizabeth's onetime best friend, the former nice but nerdy Enid Rollins, recently reborn as Alexandra.

Which left him with no Elizabeth. No basketball. Only Alexandra Rollins and the meanest, fiercest hangover of his life.

51

He looked up at a poster of Charles Barkley staring down at him. "What would *you* do?" he asked aloud.

Sir Charles had no answer.

"OK, Wilkins, get a grip. Get it together," he commanded himself. "Try to find something positive about this. Save your butt somehow." He lay on his bed, staring up at the ceiling.

"Well, number one, Elizabeth doesn't know about Alex yet," he pointed out to himself. "With any luck, she won't find out. And maybe nothing really happened last night, after all. I mean, what's a kiss or two between old pals?" He steadfastly refused to consider the scratches on his back. Innocent until proven guilty, that was his motto.

"And, OK, say the worst did happen. Say me and Alex did the wild thing. How bad could it be?" *Besides totally destroying any hope of getting back together with Elizabeth, that is.* "Enid—I mean, Alexandra—isn't bad looking," he mumbled to himself. "I mean, she *has* come a long way since high school. What's the harm in just hanging out a little bit? She's been dumped, I've been dumped. We could comfort each other." *The way you did last night?* Then a thought came to him suddenly. "I wonder what Liz would think of me and Alexandra getting it together? Would she be jealous? Would it make her wonder what she was missing?"

But he shook his head. He wanted Elizabeth back, but not that way. He wasn't that kind of guy.

Or was he?

*   *   *

Jessica walked down the Theta-house steps and turned right at the sidewalk. Her blond hair was shining in the sun, her backpack swinging from one hand. It was almost lunchtime, and she was hungry. Sighing, she decided to head back to campus to the cafeteria and eat by herself, pathetic though that would be.

She'd managed to exit the Theta house with as much style as she could muster, but the knowledge that the rest of the day yawned emptily before her was completely depressing. Elizabeth would no doubt be snorfling into Tom Terrific's neck somewhere; the Thetas were out, obviously; Mike was out, obviously. . . . What could she do with herself? Where could she go? Back to her room to study alone like a total social reject?

No unwanted guests, Alison the witch had said. Unwanted. What could make Alison change her mind about Jessica? What could Jessica—or anyone else, for that matter—do? It would take a miracle. It would take Alison getting totally out of the picture. Jessica imagined a perfect world, in which Alison Quinn had never been born. The idea brought a smile to her face.

Wham! Jessica's smile fled as she ran into a brick wall.

Well, it was a sort of wall, anyway. James Montgomery, the hunk of her chemistry class, a six-foot-three wall of steel, was standing before her, looking surprised.

"Whoa. Hey, Jessica," James said, catching her by the elbows just in time and steadying her. "Are you OK?" he asked, his hands lingering on her arms, holding her in a firm grip.

"Oh, sure, sure," Jessica said, distracted by the sunlight playing in James's eyes and hair. Objectively, Jessica knew James was good-looking. He was the guy that all the freshman girls had swooned over during orientation week. But she hadn't had an opportunity to look at him closely—until now. And this close up, Jessica could see that he was more than simply good-looking. He was gorgeous.

James's handsome face was drawn with concern. "You sure you're OK? You look a little shaken up. Here, we can sit down for a minute until you feel better."

More stunned by the perfect bone structure of James's face than the ache in her nose from running smack into him, Jessica let him lead her over toward a shady patch of grass beneath a large palm tree.

If only the Thetas could see me now, she thought dazedly. If Alison Quinn would only stick her nose out her window. This was the kind of thing that restored a girl's reputation: being seen with one of the most gorgeous and eligible guys on campus. And she, Jessica "In Disgrace" Wakefield, was doing it.

"I guess I *am* a little shaken up," Jessica admitted, leaning on James's arm as they walked to the shady spot. *Though not for the reasons you think.*

54

"Maybe I should sit down for a minute."

"I think you'd better," James said, helping her down, then sitting next to her on the grass.

As they sat there, Jessica couldn't help but notice that James had thrown an admiring glance or two in her direction as well. It was a beautiful December day, sunny and clear, with a cool, crisp breeze. She shivered a tiny bit and drew Elizabeth's blazer closer around her.

"So I suppose you're coming by to pick someone up for a date or something," Jessica probed. "Like Alison Quinn probably."

"Alison Quinn!" James laughed. "I wouldn't touch that ice queen with a ten-foot pole."

"You wouldn't?" Jessica asked, surprised, but definitely pleased, to hear his description.

"Of course not," James said. "Come on, don't look so shocked. You know how she is."

"I do?"

"Sure, you're a Theta," James said, nodding to the house behind them. "If you live with her, you must know how cold she can be. I bet she puts a freeze on the whole house."

"But I'm not a Theta," Jessica said before she could stop herself. "I . . . I was just . . . dropping off some notes for a friend," she finished weakly. *What a rotten day,* she thought, looking away from him. *Now that he knows I'm not a Theta, he probably isn't interested at all.* Nervously her fingers tugged at little blades of grass, snapping them.

"I guess you're lucky, then," James said. "You

don't have to live with Alison, after all."

Jessica looked back at him quickly. He was smiling. He definitely didn't look disappointed.

"It's probably lucky for them, too," he continued. Jessica frowned.

"No competition," he explained with an easy smile.

Jessica smiled. Maybe it wasn't such a rotten day after all.

"Actually, Jessica, I'm glad you ran into me," James said. He leaned closer, and Jessica could see the little flecks of black in his green eyes. They were mesmerizing. In the shade of the tree, his dark-chestnut hair deepened to a rich mahogany color. Jessica thought she'd never seen such gorgeous hair before.

"You are?" she breathed, looking into those eyes. Then she dropped back to earth. She had almost forgotten that she was in disgrace—that she had just gotten a marriage annulment from a notorious, dangerous guy. Probably James just needed chemistry notes or something. Well, fortunately, since she had turned into Ms. Studious, she probably had them.

"Sure. Actually, I was going to look for you today."

Jessica nodded fatalistically, waiting for him to ask her about the test on Chapter 7: "Unusual Isotopes."

"Jessica," James began, his voice taking on a serious note, "I know we haven't had the chance to get to know each other well, but I'd like that to change." He gave her a devastating smile, and Jessica's heart almost pounded out of Elizabeth's prissy blouse.

You must really need those chem notes bad, she marveled. No problem. As far as she was concerned, he could have just about anything he wanted, the gorgeous thing.

"You would?" Jessica said lamely.

"Yeah. And not just because you're the most beautiful girl on campus, either," James said. Jessica's eyes widened, and she sat up a little straighter. This kind of stuff she could listen to all day.

"But because you're an interesting person," James continued seriously. He reached out and covered one of his hands with hers.

Please, God, make Alison look out the window. She will die of jealousy. Please do just this one thing for me, God.

"What I'm trying to say, Jessica, is that you would make me very happy if you would go out with me." James's dark-green eyes looked deeply into hers. Jessica felt as if she couldn't breathe.

Trying not to scream with delight, drool, or squeal with excitement, Jessica managed to say, "A date?" With iron self-control she plastered a somewhat shy and yet pleased expression on her face.

"Yes." James took a deep breath, as though asking her out was difficult for him. "Jessica, I would love it if you came to the university New Year's party with me."

It crossed Jessica's mind that she shouldn't seem too eager. "Oh, gosh, James," she began, blushing prettily. "This is so unexpected. . . ."

James's face clouded over.

He's probably never been turned down before. And no wonder. Look at him.

"I'll tell you what," she proposed. "Why don't we have dinner tomorrow night after my big psych exam? I'll be able to think more clearly, and I'll give you my answer then. Does that sound OK?" She smiled up at him, trying to seem unsure of herself. Which wasn't too hard, actually.

James flashed her another incredible smile and took her hand, tracing his fingers across her palm. Jessica almost melted.

"It's a date, then," James said.

Jessica nodded and James stood, pulling her up next to him.

"Now, don't go running into any *other* men today," he said as he gently released her.

"I'll try not to," Jessica promised with a smile. "I don't think my nose could take another meeting like this one."

"Your nose is perfect. I'll see you tomorrow night, then." James smiled and turned to continue up the street.

"Tomorrow night," Jessica repeated dreamily. She turned back once to see if by any miracle Alison was standing shell-shocked on the porch of the Theta house, but no one was there. Oh, well. One miracle was enough for today.

Chapter Six

Tom had given up trying to study several hours earlier, around lunchtime. He sat looking out his window, nervous about the holidays. Elizabeth had already briefed him on what her parents did and didn't know about Jessica and Mike and everything that had happened over the past two months. Unfortunately, they knew almost nothing. Tom had a hard time believing it, what with Steven's being in jail for two days after the shooting, and then the public hearing. Mr. Wakefield was a lawyer, and if he'd been home, there would have been no way to keep it from him. But Mr. and Mrs. Wakefield had been on a cruise, and apparently they had missed everything. All the chaos. All the tears. All the bad press.

And even though they had just arrived back home, Tom was still amazed that no one had mentioned anything to them. Any passerby, any neighbor, any colleague who had heard *anything* could blow the lid off the whole secret with a single comment.

Tom just shook his head. He chalked it up to the twins' ingenuity. Elizabeth had warned him about not making any gaffes, letting information slip by.

"We'll just wow them with stories about *you*. Tell them about how you tracked down the society's secret meeting place and led the police there," Elizabeth had coached him.

"Great," Tom said aloud now in his room. "I'll be on display like a show dog. Sit, Tom. Roll over, Tom. Good Tom. Good boy."

Tom laughed at himself sadly.

And now he not only had to be on display for her parents, but he had to escort Elizabeth to her high-school reunion, too. Out of the frying pan and into the fire. To him it felt like an ambush, like walking into enemy territory. Elizabeth's past was a jungle, and he was a naive explorer in uncharted lands. He could see it all: a gym full of strangers parting to make way, faces peering at him, looking him up and down, scoring him: looks, six; posture, six; neatness, four. Mediocre. Nope, not good enough for her. He could hear the voices, the hushed whispers: Where's *Todd*? Who's *that* guy?

"Todd, ugh," Tom muttered. What was it with him, anyway? He'd been acting so weird lately around Elizabeth. What really bothered Tom was that Todd still had the power to ruin Elizabeth's day. Elizabeth had a heart the size of L.A. It was one of the things he loved most about her. But it was also one of his biggest sources of worry. If Todd was unhappy, Elizabeth still got unhappy. It was that simple.

Tom didn't trust him. He was definitely up to something. But what?

Stacks of textbooks towered over both sides of Alexandra's desk like craggy valley walls. She'd been sitting in the center of them for two hours now—without cracking a single one.

She took another dry Saltine cracker and nibbled it absentmindedly. In front of her was a sheet of paper with two columns. Alexandra's tally: Todd yes, Todd no. Does he want me? Do I want him? Is this good? Is this bad? Tell Elizabeth? Don't tell Elizabeth?

I never knew romance could get this complex, she thought. *Or this technical. Who am I kidding? I don't even know if it's a romance. Maybe it's just a friendship, despite the telltale signs. Or maybe*—her nose wrinkled in disgust—*maybe it's just been sex.* That was a totally depressing thought.

Tapping her pencil eraser against her forehead, she squeezed her eyes shut. "What do I feel?"

She knew she liked Todd. Maybe she'd liked him all these years—more than she'd thought. He'd always been off-limits: her best friend's boyfriend. But now Alexandra had no best friend, and Todd was single. It was food for thought. She

61

hated to admit it, but part of her had always been envious of Elizabeth. All the years they had been best friends, she'd felt as if she'd been in Elizabeth's shadow. Elizabeth was beautiful, and not only that, she was smart and genuinely caring. What chance had Alexandra had? Since coming to college, Alexandra had determinedly plowed her way into the light. Maybe being with Todd was part of that. She didn't know.

But what happened last night? I can't decide until I know for sure. It's so gross that something that "big" might have happened without my remembering it. After all, Mark was the only guy I've ever been with. And I loved him.

She thought of all those films and posters the university's health and social services had shown them during orientation week about drinking and fooling around. If you do one, don't do the other, they urged. Drinking confuses you, you can't think, you often regret what you say and do. That's what they said, and they were right.

"Were they ever," she muttered.

She straightened in her chair. *OK, so what if we did sleep together? If we did, then we have to deal with it. Decide what to do, or not to do. Together.*

Taking a deep breath, summoning her courage, Alexandra reached for the phone and dialed Todd's number. One ring . . . two rings . . . three . . . He wasn't there. Just as she was about to hang up, Todd finally answered.

"Hello?" He sounded subdued and headachy.

So they had that much in common.

Without even thinking Alexandra quickly dropped the phone back onto the cradle. She just couldn't bring herself to ask. What if he hated her? What if he had just been using her as a substitute for the blond goddess? Alexandra lay down on her bed and hugged her pillow. Sometimes love and friendship just hurt way too much.

"God, I *hate* it when people do that," Todd said as he put down the phone and collapsed into his bed. It was almost dinnertime, but he wasn't hungry. After last night he thought he'd never be able to face food again. He certainly wouldn't be able to face Scotch.

Putting his hands behind his head, he gazed up at the ceiling. After going over last night in his mind again and again, he'd decided that he and Alexandra definitely had not slept together. He'd been able to account for every hour. Everything was blurry, but there weren't any blanks.

But the burden wasn't gone. He still had a headache, and he felt as though an elephant were sitting on his chest. There was something else wrong. And that something was *everything*. His entire life was unraveling. This potential disaster with Alex was just a symptom, a clue. He needed to talk to someone, and fast. But his best friend and teammate Mark Gathers had left SVU a few weeks ago.

For about half a minute he considered calling

Lauren, but his relationship with her seemed a million years behind him. He tried to remember the details, what Lauren wore, her perfume, what she felt like in his arms. Her memory had already faded. During the hearings with the dean, he'd thought she'd bailed out on him. Since he'd lost his eligibility—and his position as one of the team's stars—it wasn't as if she'd been knocking down his door, seeing if he was OK, trying to make up. All he could think was that she'd been in it only for herself, that she didn't care about him. Now some mechanism in his brain had shut off his memory of her, out of anger and pain.

He was certain that it was a sign that Lauren was wrong for him. But wasn't it also a sign that Elizabeth was right? He had no problem remembering everything about her. Hell, if he thought about her hard enough, he could practically see her, feel her, right next to him.

On a sudden impulse Todd reached for his phone and dialed Elizabeth's number.

The phone rang and rang. Then suddenly the realization came over him like a black cloud, and he hung up: Elizabeth was with Watts. She'd made it clear to Todd after that secret-society business that she didn't want to see him or talk to him. She would be his friend, but that was all. And hardly even his friend, he thought bitterly.

Swallows were singing loudly in the trees outside the open window, but to Todd they sounded like a cloud of screeching crows. He got up and slammed the window shut.

He looked around his room. After his suspension he'd taken down all his basketball mementos, his high-school trophies, his old uniforms. He'd put away his shoes, his sweats. Anything that reminded him of basketball. Except the poster of his inspiration, Sir Charles. Charles Barkley wasn't only an awesome player, he was a solid human being, an honest man unafraid of saying what he felt. Todd respected that. He wanted to be more like that. More like a complete man, not just a ball player, a money machine, a dumb jock who took illegal handouts to play. He wanted to prove he deserved the attention, but instead he had been suspended.

That seemed to be the central theme in his life: Just when he was ready to produce, to do the right thing, it was too late. With basketball. With Elizabeth.

Now his room was totally bare, an anonymous cinder-block cube, just like every other dorm room at SVU. It could have been anyone's room, everyone's room, and it was. There was nothing of him in it except some clothes, some notebooks. He didn't recognize it. He didn't recognize himself, his shattered life.

Todd stared blankly at the books and notes strewn over his desk. His first big final was tomorrow, but his books looked like foreign objects. He hadn't cracked them in weeks.

Opening one, he peered in. It was four months into the semester, and reading Chapter 1 of European history was like reading Greek. It was useless. He couldn't start his school life again when school was about to end. He had to start over at the beginning. That's what he needed. A new beginning.

Pushing his books away, he stood resolutely. He went to his closet and stared in. Taking a big breath, he yanked his duffel bag out from under a clutter of socks and shoes and books. He went from drawer to drawer, turning each one over, dumping the contents into the bag. He looked at his books but decided to leave them. Where he was going, he wouldn't need them.

Standing in the middle of the floor, he took one last look around the room. *What will I remember most about it?* he asked himself. *Nothing,* he decided as he turned his back and walked out the door, not even closing it. Why bother? There was nothing left. He was dropping out, leaving SVU—for good.

"Getting out of my room was a great idea, Nina," Elizabeth said as they strolled through the quad.

Students were passing them on all sides, hurrying across the lush, grassy courtyard toward the library with their heads down as if headed into a snowstorm. Small groups of other students were sprawled on the grass, but the usual radios,

Frisbees, and touch-football games were missing. No one was catching any rays today. Everyone was surrounded by books and papers, studying desperately for finals.

Elizabeth looked around with wonder, taking it all in. She felt as if she were on a different planet, or trapped in some alien theme park. "Wow, this place really changes during exam week. I mean, this is still SVU, isn't it?"

"Yeah," Nina said with a grin. "Peace and quiet. No boom boxes blasting at four in the morning. Even the fraternity blockheads have their faces buried in books instead of mugs of beer. During exam week," Nina said, holding her arms out wide, "the whole world's a library."

Elizabeth looked at Nina as they walked through the outer gates of the quad.

"You seem so . . . I don't know . . . *driven*," Elizabeth said.

"I was only kidding, Liz." Nina turned to her with a smile.

"No, I mean it. I've never known anyone as disciplined as you are."

"That's what I tell my other friends about *you*. Until lately, that is. Until Tom came into your life and threw everything out of whack."

"But nothing distracts you," Elizabeth said, a touch of admiration creeping into her voice.

A strange look came into Nina's eyes, and her eyebrows rose. She quickly turned away from the road and ducked behind a palm tree.

"Nina, what's wrong?" Elizabeth asked, alarmed.

"Isn't that Todd's car?" Nina whispered.

Todd's BMW slowed but didn't stop. As it passed, Elizabeth saw Todd staring out the window at her with an expression she didn't recognize. Once she had known Todd so well that she could tell what he was thinking just by looking into his eyes. But since he'd dumped her for Lauren Hill, his eyes were more like smoked mirrors.

"What's with him?" she said in a low voice. The look he was giving her was so weird. She hoped he wasn't following her around again. For the past couple weeks it seemed as if wherever she was, there Todd was too, staring at her. But the look on his face now was different somehow, a strange hybrid between anger and sadness.

"Why is all his stuff piled in the back of his car?" Nina asked; then she turned slowly to look at Elizabeth.

Elizabeth was thinking the same thing, and her eyes grew wide. It was true—all Todd's stuff was loaded into his car. He was heading toward the highway, out of town. He was leaving school, and it looked as though he wasn't planning on coming back.

"Is he crazy?" Elizabeth blurted. Quickly she stepped into the street and raised her arm for him to stop. But Todd, staring straight ahead, stomped on the gas. The rear tires spun, the car lurched, and he peeled down the road in a blue cloud of burned rubber.

Elizabeth shook her head and bit her lip. Difficult questions roamed around in her head: Was he in trouble somehow? Had he been kicked out? How was it possible that they were strangers to each other, after so many years together? She thought about all the times recently he had called her but she had been too busy to talk. All the times she didn't have a minute to spend with him because she was seeing Tom. Could she have helped him somehow?

Nina stepped into the road and looked with Elizabeth down the road. "What was that all about?" she asked.

"I'm not sure," Elizabeth said as the last of the smoke drifted away.

"Where's he going?"

Elizabeth felt her eyes moisten. "I don't know. Away from here, I guess." *Away from me,* she finished her thought.

Nina shook her head. "That's one confused boy."

"Do you think I did anything wrong, Nina?"

"Wrong?"

"You know. Did I let him down gently enough? Was I hard on him?"

Nina stared at her. "Girl, are you nuts? What world are you living in? You're forgetting something, aren't you? Todd dumped *you*. Two seconds later he was tangled up with Lauren Hill. And now you're standing here going, 'Was I hard on

69

him?'" She mimicked Elizabeth's voice. "The question should be, was he hard on *you*?"

Elizabeth sighed and pushed her long hair back over her shoulder. "You're right, you're right. But I don't know, Nina. I can't just turn my back on him. We were together for a long time. Maybe when the semester started he was just . . ."

"Just what?" Nina said testily. "Bored? Stupid? Personally, I vote for 'stupid.' Look, Liz." Nina put a comforting arm around Elizabeth's shoulders. "You did what anyone in your shoes would do. You moved on with your life. You've decided to be happy. I don't know about you, but in my book happiness is a good thing."

Elizabeth turned to her. "You're right, Nina," she said again, wiping away a single tear with the back of her hand. "I'm fine. I really am. I feel sorry for Todd, but . . . but I really don't miss him. We both have to get on with our lives. He made his choices, and I've made mine."

"Now you're talking. Come on—the clock is ticking, and we have some heavy-duty studying to do."

"With any luck I won't flunk out," Elizabeth groaned.

"Flunk out? Of this place?" Nina laughed, lassoing Elizabeth's arm and dragging her across the road. "You're not flunking out of anything. Not as long as I'm around."

Chapter Seven

"Quick, what time is it?" Jessica called, checking her makeup in the bathroom mirror.

Elizabeth glanced at the clock on her desk. "Almost six thirty. I guess I better be heading over to the cafeteria to meet Nina for dinner."

"Ta-da. What do you think?" Jessica swirled out of the bathroom and posed dramatically in the doorway. For this all-important date with James, she had chosen her outfit carefully. Her black velvet catsuit clung to her like her own skin, and the short black embroidered bolero jacket showed off her narrow waist. Soft black leather boots were on her feet, and her long blond hair made a striking contrast with her jacket.

"Good Lord," Elizabeth said. "He won't know what hit him. I hope you know what you're doing."

Jessica rolled her eyes, then swept her hair over her shoulder so she could fasten her dangly gold earrings. "Liz, please. It's my first date in who

71

knows how long. Every other guy on campus has been scared off by my ugly marriage and uglier annulment." She practiced tilting her head in the mirror, making her earrings swing. "I thought I'd never date again. And to be dating *James Montgomery*—well, let's just say I'm making a stunning recovery," she said smugly.

At her desk Elizabeth laughed. "I guess you're right. You deserve to have fun after what you've been through."

"Too right," Jessica agreed. "Besides, I did great on my psych exam. It was the first time in my life that I actually knew the answers to a test."

"It must have been totally disorienting," Elizabeth teased. "But seriously, Jess, it's all that studying you've been doing. It's all paying off. Isn't it a good feeling?"

"Yeah," Jessica admitted, shining the tip of her boot with Elizabeth's bedspread.

"So you think you'll keep it up? Next semester you could try for the dean's list."

Stopping in midbuff, Jessica stared at her sister. "Are you insane? Studying this hard has been a total nightmare. You know I'm only doing it to rehabilitate my reputation. But once I'm back in the Thetas, it's going to be *par-ty* time!" Jessica raised her arms over her head and did a little shimmy.

"You're too much," Elizabeth said, shaking her head.

Jessica went to the window, looked out, and immediately squealed. "There he is! He's got a red

Mazda Miata! I better take a scarf. See you later, Liz! Wish me luck." Whirling, she turned and flew out the door.

"Good luck," Elizabeth offered to her parting back.

As she ran down the dorm stairs, Jessica's heart was galloping with excitement. When she reached the lobby, she slowed to a stately walk, calmed her breathing, and carefully tied the red chiffon scarf around her hair, Grace Kelly style. Things were finally looking up for her. Girls from the Thetas were at least talking to her, her grades were picking up at least for the time being, and now that Mike was out of the picture, she had a date with the most fabulous guy on campus. And he had a totally hot car.

Cool it, Jessica, she reminded herself as she pushed open the lobby door. *Don't seem too eager.* She'd never forgotten what Bruce Patman had told her in high school. For men the fun of dating was the chase—going after the girl relentlessly until she gave in. No matter what they said, they liked the challenge, the adventure.

James got out of the car and strode up the walk toward her with a single red rose in his hand. She could feel his eyes admiring her as he approached. A tiny purr of satisfaction began deep in her throat as she saw him take in her outfit with undeniable approval.

James, meanwhile, wore just what Jessica had chosen for him in her mind: an olive linen blazer, white T-shirt, jeans, and cowboy boots. Jessica

73

almost melted when she saw him. If only Alison Quinn could see her now.

"You look . . . gorgeous," James said, seeming kind of overwhelmed.

Jessica smiled modestly and blushed; then James held open the car door and she slid inside.

In the driver's seat James turned and faced her. He gently tucked a blond strand beneath her scarf. "So. Tonight was your idea," he said softly. "Where am I taking you?"

Jessica knew exactly where she wanted to go. Three hours ago she'd aced her psych exam. Now she wanted to see if she could pass another test.

"How about El Capitano?" she said. El Capitano was where Mike had taken her on their first formal date. It was on the beach and had a patio that looked out over the water, as well as an elegant dining room. It was chic and expensive, and when she had been there with Mike, she'd felt as if they were masquerading, playing king and queen for the night. But James was the real thing: rich, smart, and sophisticated. Jessica wanted to prove to herself that she was over Mike by going there with James. She wanted to sit at a linen-covered table and gaze into James's eyes all night. She was determined to pass this test with flying colors.

"El Capitano is exactly what I was thinking," James said as he turned the key in the ignition. "They have great food."

As the low-slung car headed down the street, James turned up the volume on the CD player.

Beautiful, haunting violins melted into the night air and enveloped Jessica in a shroud of excitement. Suddenly she felt as if she were enchanted, or the evening were enchanted. The effect was magical.

"Do you like it?" James asked, smiling over at her. Since it was December, it had been dark for several hours. His hair looked as dark as wine in the night air, and his eyes were almost black.

Jessica nodded dreamily. Most of the guys she'd dated listened to modern stuff—whatever was popular. She thought James was incredibly sophisticated to play something classical.

In a few minutes he expertly swung the small car into the parking lot of El Capitano. He got out, tossed the keys to the parking valet, and opened Jessica's door for her. Then they were under the red awning and pushing through the glass doors.

As James walked Jessica in, a twinge of nostalgia for Mike ambushed her. She pictured the exact moment when she'd been there with him. It seemed like a lifetime ago.

The maître d' led them through the restaurant and out onto the patio, where large, radiant heaters took the chill off the night. They were seated at a small table for two overlooking the water. Jessica could hear the waves lapping gently at the columns beneath the patio.

A waiter brought James a menu, but he held up a restraining hand. "To start, I think we'll have the buffalo mozzarella with fresh tomato and basil," he said authoritatively. "And a bottle of the Beaujolais nouveau."

"As you like, sir," the waiter said, and spun away.

Jessica breathed in the cool, salty sea air. She shook out her hair gently, letting it fall over her shoulders. The lights of far-off boats winked on the horizon like a new constellation of stars.

"So," James said, leaning across the table and gazing into Jessica's blue-green eyes. "We're here, just like you wanted. Now, how about an answer to my question? Will you be my date at the SVU New Year's party?"

It was all Jessica could do not to blurt out "Yes!" and leap across the table at him.

She looked out at the water. "Hmm, well, I don't know."

James sat back, disappointment drying up his gleaming smile.

"I mean, some things need to be thought over," Jessica said coyly. "I tell you what—I'll make you a deal."

Interest sparked in James's dark-green eyes. "I like making deals," he said in a low voice.

Jessica's smile dimpled. "I'll be your date at the New Year's party, if . . . you'll be my date at my high-school reunion the day after Christmas."

James sat back, still looking deeply into her eyes. "High-school reunions can be pretty heavy, you know," he said. "Who you bring . . . it says everything you want to say, doesn't it?"

"Yes," Jessica said meaningfully. "It does."

She could feel the air over the table buzz with electricity. Everything sparkled: the china, the crystal tulip glasses, the silverware.

"It's very symbolic," James continued. "Everyone you know will be there. You sure it's me you want to go with?"

Jessica lowered her lashes demurely. This was going better than she'd expected. "I know a good thing when I see it," she said.

"I do too. But is that what you want?"

Jessica's eyes met his again. "It's all I want."

It was late, but Mike forced himself to press the weights forward one more time. His legs shook with the strain, but he gritted his teeth and pushed hard with his feet, moving the footpad away. Finally he stopped, drenched with sweat, and rested for a moment.

A male physical therapist came in, carrying a clipboard. "You still here, man? You have to be careful not to overdo it. You've lost muscle mass in the last few weeks. Bring it back slowly."

"Yeah, OK," Mike muttered, gulping from his bottle of water. With the therapist's help he stood, and the therapist pushed Mike's walker closer to him. Mike gripped the sides securely, feeling the heaviness of his feet, the soreness of his legs. He grinned. He would rather feel burning pain all the time rather than nothing. Every hour that passed seemed to bring more sensation to his legs. He could feel the spongy resistance of the exercise mat as he headed awkwardly for the door of the rehab center.

Everything about life was fresh and exciting. These new, geeky white sneakers, the sweat running off his body, the hunger he felt not just for food, but for all of life, good and bad. Even the elevator music piped into the rehab center, sweeping over him, a sappy song he'd heard a thousand times and always hated, now sounded innovative and eye-opening. He hummed along. He had a new lease on life. A second chance.

Outside he made his way clumsily to the patients' van that would take him back to his apartment. Two other motility-impaired patients were already waiting. With a supreme effort Mike picked up first one foot, then the other, and clambered inside. Flopping back on a bench seat, he folded his walker and pulled it in after him. It was the first thing he'd done for himself in a long, long time. But that was how it was going to be from now on, he told himself. Now that he was definitely on the road to recovery, he was going to do everything himself, be independent again, like before.

It was a whole new beginning, in more ways than one. He'd changed, changed for the better. He'd learned a lot about himself, and about other people, since the shooting. He'd grown up a lot. In the last two days, since the incident with Steven and the gas, Mike had done a lot of thinking. Now he could see what a jerk he'd been to Jessica. The thought almost tore him in two. She'd been the best thing that had ever happened to him, and he'd thrown her away. What a creep.

As the van rolled through the hills of the town, he let his mind drift back, back to when he'd first seen Jessica, first met her. She'd been the most beautiful girl he'd ever seen in his life. Hell, she still was. From the very beginning, though, the course of true love had run anything but smoothly. She'd intimidated him, made him nervous. She was so fine, and he was such a loser, though he knew now that she hadn't thought so. But he had. He remembered their first date—he'd brought her to the fanciest place he could think of. El Capitano. What a mistake. She'd looked completely at home there; he'd felt completely out of place. It had been a little tense—she'd rolled her eyes when he'd drunk his beer out of the bottle. After dinner they'd taken a walk along the beach, then watched a video in his apartment they hadn't really paid much attention to.

As usual he'd been in a hurry, sure that this beautiful girl was going to melt out of his life if he let her go for a second. It had taken some doing, but he'd finally gotten her to spend the night. Mike tightened his grip on his walker as he remembered the feel of her in his arms, her silky skin, her shower of golden hair, her bottomless blue-green eyes . . .

Now she was gone. After all, she wasn't a fool. Of course she'd dumped him. He'd left her no choice. But his anger at her and at the situation had drained away as soon as there had been a tingle of feeling in his legs. He'd been given another chance. Life itself was saying, "Take another shot." And now everything was going to be better than it had been before. He was going to get it together, get his old life back. This time he was going to do it right. And the first thing on his list, the most important goal, the biggest wrong he had to make right, was Jessica.

Alexandra slammed down the telephone. Todd had been incommunicado for two days. Ever since she'd woken up the day before, she'd been eager to talk to him, find out what was going on, what had happened. But he hadn't been around all yesterday, or all today, either. She'd stopped by his room after her history final, but he hadn't been there. Feeling a desperation and a seething anger at his desertion, she'd called everyone she could think of: the gym, the cafeteria, Todd's teammates. No one had seen Todd. No one had heard from him.

There was one last hope. If he wasn't going to talk to her, she knew he would at least talk to his parents sometime. It would unnerve him to get a message from her through them. It would embarrass him. Good.

She dialed directory assistance for the town of Sweet Valley, then punched in the number for the Wilkinses' residence. One ring . . . two . . . three . . . wasn't anyone there, either? What was with these people?

"Hello?"

At first Alexandra couldn't utter a sound. She felt as if someone had just dumped ice water down her shirt. It was *Todd*. At his parents' house in Sweet Valley, in the middle of finals. What was going on? She hadn't realized just how much she'd wanted to talk to him until she heard his voice.

"Todd, is that you?"

"Who's this?"

"Alex*an*dra."

An awkward silence deadened the phone line.

"Alexandra *Rollins*," she said sarcastically.

"Yeah, hi, Alex," Todd answered in an unenthusiastic monotone.

"Hi, *Alex*? Is that all you can say to me?" For two days she'd been desperate to talk to him, to hear his voice, to be reassured, and this is what she got?

"What do you want me to say?"

Alexandra was about ready to cry. "Todd, why are you in Sweet Valley? You have finals. You had one today. Didn't you take it? Has something happened at home?" Maybe that was why he was being so weird. If something awful had happened, she would forgive him. If not, he was in deep doo-doo.

"I dropped out, Alex," Todd said in a clipped voice.

"Dropped *out*?" Alexandra said in shock. "Why?"

"Alex, I can't really talk right now. How about if I call you later—"

"Wait, Todd!" Her mind was whirling, thinking, going through all the possibilities.

81

There was a long, suspended silence.

"What?" Todd finally mumbled.

"I've been trying to reach you since yesterday. I felt . . . like we really needed to talk about . . . you know."

Silence. She was starting to hate him.

"I want to know . . ." she pushed on bravely, fueled by anger. "I mean, I *need* to know. Did we . . . do you think we . . ."

Alexandra heard Todd cough on the other end of the line. She felt her own face heat up with embarrassment.

"No," Todd replied flatly. "I'm pretty sure we didn't. I think . . . I think we'd know."

Alexandra thought she'd feel relief. But now she wasn't sure what she felt.

"We came close, though," Todd added.

"Well . . . well, maybe it wouldn't have been such a bad thing," she said, trying to get some response out of him.

Todd didn't answer for a long time. It felt like hours. She could hear him breathing.

"Maybe not," he finally said.

Alexandra felt a smile creep across her face. She leaned against her desk and felt her grip on the phone relax a little bit.

"So, what about the reunion?" Todd said, breaking into her thoughts.

"Reunion? Oh, I wasn't going to go. I mean, why bother?" *Why bother putting myself through the humiliation?*

"I know what you mean." Todd sounded almost bitter. "So, I mean, if you weren't going to go, and I wasn't going to go, why don't we just go together?"

Alexandra's eyebrows shot up. "Yeah? Really?"

"Why not?"

Half of Alexandra couldn't help but wonder why Todd asked her, but the other half was too elated to worry about it.

"Great. That would be great . . . I . . ." Alexandra trailed off, imagining walking into the gym on Todd Wilkins's arm, everyone's expressions, the surprise, the jealousy.

I'll show them, she thought. *I'll be Todd Wilkins's date.* It would be her final assurance that she'd outgrown her reputation; that she'd finally put the old *Enid* to rest for good.

"So I'll pick you up at your house at seven," Todd said. "The day after Christmas."

"Great!" She could hardly contain her excitement. "Oh, and . . . uh, Todd? The other night . . . well, I'm sort of glad it happened."

She could hear Todd struggling for something to say. "Me too," he finally said, as if he wasn't sure he meant it.

But it hardly mattered. Alexandra was going to the Sweet Valley High reunion on his arm. After she hung up, she held the receiver to her cheek, in her mind's eye picturing dancing across the gym floor. Elizabeth and Tom. Her and Todd. She heard the whispering, the talk, the comments.

The holidays were shaping up, after all.

83

Chapter Eight

Lila leaned back against the chintz sofa cushions in the living room of the Theta house. She was bored. Most of the Thetas were either out taking their finals or in their rooms anxiously cramming. Since Lila was only auditing courses, she had no need to do either. But now there was no one to talk to.

Sighing, she turned the pages of the spring-semester course book, marking which classes looked interesting. As a freshman she didn't need to declare a major, but she thought it would be efficient to focus on something right away.

The front door opened, then shut with a slam as a quick gust of wintry breeze pulled it closed. Moments later Alison Quinn appeared in the living room, shrugging off her leather blazer.

"Hi, Lila," the older girl greeted her.

Lila smiled back. She didn't really like Alison, especially since she was being so hateful to Jessica.

But Alison was the president of the Thetas, and therefore, she was useful. There was no need to antagonize her. Besides, Lila knew that Alison liked *her*, and it was hard not to enjoy that.

Alison stood in front of the fireplace, which had a warm, crackling blaze in it. "It's a little nippy out there," she said conversationally.

"But it's lovely in here," Lila said. "I was just about to make a nice pot of tea. Would you like some?"

"Sure," Alison said, following her to the Theta kitchen. "You know, Lila, I'm glad to see how comfortable you are here. You really fit in well with the Thetas. You belong here."

Shooting Alison a quick glance to check her sincerity, Lila decided she probably meant it. Alison might be eager to have Lila for a member if for no other reason than to get Jessica's goat bigtime. Which, of course, it would.

"Thanks," Lila said easily, putting a brightly polished copper kettle on the burner. "I like it here. I'm looking forward to moving in if and when I become a Theta. It's a drag always having to commute back and forth from Sweet Valley. In fact, I was thinking about trying to get an apartment soon, close to campus. Then, when next semester starts, I'll be all set."

Alison smiled and took the tea out of the cupboard. "Well, I know I can speak for the other sisters as well as myself when I say that I don't think you'll have to be in your apartment for long." She shook some tea into a wire strainer. "Oh, guess who I just ran into? Bruce Patman. You went to high school with him, didn't you?"

Lila made a face. "Ugh. Don't remind me."

"What do you mean?" Alison looked interested. "He's one of the hottest guys on campus."

"He certainly thinks he is," Lila agreed, pouring out the boiling water.

"Oh, come on," Alison said. "He's just confident. That's incredibly attractive in a guy. What's so bad about him, anyway? I mean, he's gorgeous, sure of himself, rich, and God knows he's got a great body. Where's the catch?"

"Nowhere, as long as he doesn't open his mouth."

Alison laughed.

Lila thought for a moment while she dunked the tea strainer up and down. OK, anyone who knew Bruce Patman hated him. Or at least most people did. For example, she did. Jessica did. Elizabeth did. Lila smirked to herself as she recalled that during high school both Jessica *and* Elizabeth had fallen prey to the deadly Patman charm. Their flings hadn't lasted long, but they were blots on the Wakefields' date books. Lila still prided herself on never having succumbed. But here was Alison Quinn, president of the Thetas, practically drooling into her teacup over him. Go figure. However, Alison's interest could be useful to Lila. After all, she *did* know Bruce. They did *speak* to each other. And though her acceptance

86

into the Thetas was pretty much a sure thing, insurance never hurt, as her dad always said.

"Yeah, ol' Bruce is a maniac," Lila said, trying to sound affectionate.

"He is?" Alison asked eagerly. "In what way?"

"Well, he's the kind of guy who *eats* life, if you know what I mean," Lila said, taking the tea tray back into the living room. "He always said he wanted to live fast, die young, and leave a good-looking corpse." *Bruce is real original that way.*

"Wow." Alison laughed.

"You know, he's younger than you," Lila pointed out.

Alison shrugged. "Who cares? He looks older than his age, and he's still hotter than a lot of seniors." She slowly stirred sugar into her tea. "Have you ever been out with him?"

They don't make enough Pepto-Bismol for me to try it. "Actually, no," Lila said, trying to look modest. "I mean, he's asked me out a bunch of times, but I've always seemed to have something better to do." *Especially since I try to coordinate my nail polish to my outfit. That takes a lot of time.*

Alison's eyebrows rose. "Better than going out with Bruce Patman?" She sounded skeptical.

Lila smiled sheepishly. Or at least she hoped it looked sheepish. She'd have to practice later in a mirror. "Yeah, well . . . he's asked me to go flying with him. Maybe I will." *You may turn green with jealousy now, Alison. I give you my permission.*

"Really?" Alison looked impressed.

But as much as Lila was enjoying torturing Alison with hints about Bruce, as soon as she'd mentioned flying, an uneasy feeling had come over her. Her nightmare came back to her all over again, as though it were happening right in front of her. Again she saw the small plane smashing into the side of the snowy mountain, then bursting into flames. What did it mean? her mind screamed. What was happening to her?

I've got to remember never to take advanced torts again, Steven promised himself as he left his apartment and headed downstairs. *Not only is it the most boring subject known to man, but the exam is a double whammy: intensely soporific and completely incomprehensible.* He'd just finished his last exam of the semester, for which he'd dropped to his knees and given thanks in the privacy of his apartment. Or almost privacy. Billie hadn't been able to stop laughing at him.

Steven grinned. Things with Billie were going well again. It was like old times. During Jessica's marriage to Mike, Steven had been so concerned and furious that he'd almost ruined his own relationship. Billie had actually moved out for a while. Then, during the trial after the shooting, he'd found out just how loyal she really was. Now they were more in love than ever. He'd left her upstairs, packing their things to go to the Wakefields' for Christmas.

But first he had something to do: He had a

Christmas present for Mike, and he wanted to deliver it in person. He'd seen Mike almost every day since their exciting adventure in the world of gas poisoning, and their relationship had changed subtly. Before, they'd flat-out hated each other's guts. But now things were different. Mike was different. Saving Steven's life and getting some feeling back in his legs had changed him somehow. Steven could actually stand to be in the same room with the guy. Just the night before, he'd hung out with Mike for a couple hours, drinking a beer while Mike did his rehab exercises. It had been weird to think they were doing voluntarily what each of them had been ordered to do by the court. Not that the court had ordered Steven to drink beer, he amended.

Reaching Mike's apartment, he leaned on the doorbell. "Whatsa matter?" he yelled when Mike didn't answer right away. "You a cripple or something?"

The door swung open, and Mike gave Steven a look that was half-amused and half–pissed off. "Why don't you yell a little louder?" he said. "I think the people in 4D didn't hear you."

Grinning, Steven pushed his way in and shrugged off his jacket. Mike moved back to his spot on the couch. In only four days his abilities had progressed tremendously. Now he could walk for short distances without falling flat on his butt. He still used the walker for longer distances. But he was being a demon about doing his exercises.

He was totally determined to get back to being a hundred percent fit. Then he could approach Jessica again.

"So what's up?" Mike asked. "Want a beer?"

Steven shook his head. "I'm going to be driving in a little while—heading home for the holidays."

Mike nodded and flicked off the TV with his remote.

"Anyway, I have a little something for you," Steven said, feeling suddenly self-conscious.

"A gift? For *moi*?" Mike said, feigning shock.

"Yeah. Here." Steven thrust the heavy package at Mike, who almost dropped it in surprise.

"Let me guess. It's a bowling ball. In case I ever join the wheelchair league."

Steven made a wry face. "Another few days and you wouldn't be eligible," he pointed out.

"Yeah." Mike grinned. "That's true." Looking awkward, he hesitantly tore off the paper wrapping. There were several layers of Christmas wrap and several more layers of brown paper underneath. "Is this stuff nuclear waste or something?" Mike asked with mock suspicion. He tore off another layer of paper, wrestling with it in his lap.

"Need help?" Steven asked innocently.

Mike glared at him. "*No*. I can do it myself. But here's a Christmas tip, Wakefield. Next time let the little woman do the wrapping." Finally he tore off the last piece of paper, then stared at the object. His eyes lit up and he burst out laughing.

"A doorstop! Great. Just what I needed. I seem to have misplaced the one I had."

Steven laughed too. "I saw it and I thought of you," he said honestly. It was a heavy cast-iron doorstop of a jackass.

"It's perfect," Mike said, putting it heavily on the coffee table. "You never know when you might have to heave one through a window."

Steven laughed again.

"I have something for you too," Mike admitted.

Steven's eyebrows rose in surprise, and he waited while Mike moved slowly to the bedroom to return with a package.

"Here, Merry Christmas," he said, handing it to Steven. "I had the store wrap it," he pointed out helpfully.

"Very nice." Steven made an oohing and aahing face, then ripped the paper open. Inside the box was a T-shirt with the words: "Powered by Natural Gas."

He looked up into Mike's eyes, and they both cracked up.

"I thought it was appropriate," Mike snorted. "Since you're going to be a lawyer and all."

Steven doubled over laughing.

By five o'clock on the last day of exams, student-packed cars were pouring out of the SVU campus parking lots. One of them was Steven's old Volkswagen Beetle, full of bodies and luggage.

91

"Hey, get your elbow out of my face," Elizabeth complained.

"I would if Jessica would get her foot off my knee," Tom said apologetically.

The backseat of Steven's car was a tangle of arms and legs so thick it was hard to tell what belonged to whom. The driver's seat was shoved so far forward that Steven's chin rode the top of the steering wheel. The only one who was comfortable was Billie, in the other front seat, while Elizabeth and Jessica squirmed for room, pinched in a tight sandwich around Tom.

"Homeward!" Steven cried. "One semester closer to law school!" For the fourth time he started singing his Christmas-carol medley, beginning with *"Oh, come, all ye faithful . . ."*

"Give us a break!" Jessica cried, clamping her hands over her ears.

"Come on, Jessica, get with the Christmas spirit," Billie said with a wicked grin. Then Steven hit a high note, and she recoiled. "Honey, maybe you should stop," she suggested calmly.

"Joyful and triumphant," Steven warbled happily.

Groaning, Elizabeth laid her head on Tom's shoulder. She couldn't believe the semester was over. It felt as if it had lasted much longer than four months. So many things had happened. As she peered out the window, watching the SVU campus pass by, she wanted to shout with relief. The last few days all she had dreamed about was this moment, when she'd be on her way home, leaving behind the trauma of final exams and her forced exile away from Tom.

"Thank *God* it's over!" she said, squeezing Tom's arm. "I never thought I'd make it through."

Tom looked down and gave her a special, private smile. "No kidding," he said in her ear. "Now we have to make up for lost time."

She smiled and curled up closer to him so they could kiss.

Steven peered at the three of them in his rear-view mirror. "So, kids, did we all pass our exams?"

Elizabeth and Tom broke apart and exchanged smiles.

"After the sacrifices I made, I better have," Elizabeth said.

"I actually don't know. The last several days are just a foggy blur in my mind," Tom said.

Elizabeth looked across Tom at Jessica. Her twin sister was looking out the window, smiling a secret little smile, keeping her thoughts to herself.

"What about you, Jess? How'd you make out?"

"Oh, OK, I guess," she replied nonchalantly.

Elizabeth waited for Jessica to rant about how silly English was, and how psychologists were just old men with beards who liked to hear themselves talk. She waited to hear that the only reason Jessica took chemistry was to meet cute future doctors. But it didn't come. Instead Jessica just stared out the window in silent contentment. Like someone who'd just aced her exams.

Jessica? Ace her exams? No way.

"So I overheard Isabella talking about the psych exam. She said the multiple choice was a killer," Elizabeth probed. "Do you really think you did well?" The night of her date with James, she'd been floating on air, but maybe reality had set in by now.

"No, it was fine," Jessica replied calmly.

"How about chem?"

"Not really. Pretty easy."

Elizabeth caught Steven's glance in the rearview mirror, and they exchanged exaggerated shocked looks.

"Who are you, and what have you done with the real Jessica?" Steven demanded. Everyone laughed.

"I'm really happy for you, Jess," Elizabeth said. "You've worked so hard these past few weeks. I hope it paid off for you."

Just then Steven cleared his throat. "I guess you're wondering why I called you all here," he said jokingly, but then his expression sobered. "But actually we have some things to talk about." He downshifted and headed the Beetle onto the on ramp of the highway toward Sweet Valley.

Jessica's smile vanished. A hush fell over the car. Elizabeth felt a tension coiling in the pit of her stomach. She knew they had to deal with it, but she wished they didn't.

"Mom and Dad don't know anything," Steven said, jumping right in.

Elizabeth knew he was talking about Jessica and Mike: their marriage, their annulment, the shooting, Steven's two days in jail. . . . It was inevitable. With all that had happened, what were they going to do about it?

"It's a miracle they haven't heard," Steven continued. "But so far, it looks like they haven't. I haven't heard a peep out of them about it."

"Good. Let's just keep it that way," Jessica said tensely. An embarrassed flush stained her cheeks, and she shifted to look out the window. Night was falling rapidly, and the streetlamps made odd patterns on her face.

"Well, Jess, I usually think honesty is the best policy, but in this case I have to agree," Steven said, glancing back in the mirror.

Everyone looked at Elizabeth. She had done a lot of thinking about the whole thing, and though she hated deceiving her parents, she couldn't really see the benefit of telling them. After all, it was over and done with. Everyone just wanted to forget about it. "Me too," she said. "I guess."

"You know they'd kill me if they ever found out," Jessica said. "And I just want to forget it ever happened. I want it to be like a nightmare that I've woken up from and never have to have again."

Elizabeth felt a pang in her heart when she heard Jessica's voice crack.

"It's going to take a lot of cooperation," Steven said. "Among all of us."

"And a lot of lying," Elizabeth couldn't help murmuring.

"Liz!" Jessica seemed near tears.

"Don't worry, Jessica," Elizabeth said quickly. "They won't hear it from me."

"We're all going to have to be alert," Steven said, sounding like a platoon commander delivering marching orders. "We all have to have the same stories. If one of us makes a slip and gets in trouble, the others have to come to that person's aid. We have to stick together. Agreed?"

"Agreed," everyone replied in unison.

"What happens when they find out from someone else?" Tom asked dryly. "Don't you think it's only a matter of time?"

"We'll deal with that when we have to," Jessica snapped. "Right now I just want to enjoy being home for the holidays, OK?"

"OK," Tom said, spreading his hands and shrugging.

"It feels weird keeping something so big from them," Elizabeth said soberly.

"That's because it isn't about you," Jessica asserted. "If you were trying to hide a huge, horrible secret, it would feel real normal. Maybe not normal," she amended. "But definitely worthwhile."

"Maybe so," Elizabeth agreed.

"Like, for instance, if you were going to have a sex-change operation, Elizabeth," Steven suggested helpfully. "We would back *you* up, wouldn't we, Jessica?"

Tom snorted, and Jessica gave Steven a fed-up look.

Billie glanced at Steven. "Does this mean I shouldn't spill the beans about your dropping law and running away to clown school?" she asked innocently.

Elizabeth and Tom were both laughing by now.

"Law school, clown school, what's the difference?" Tom asked cheerfully.

"Watch it, Watts," Steven said darkly. "You're not in the family yet."

"Go on, everybody," Jessica said in a hurt voice. "Joke. Have a laugh at my expense. My life is in shreds, and all you can do is make it a punch line."

Elizabeth leaned across Tom and took Jessica's hand. "We're just tense, Jessica," she said soothingly. "We're just trying to lighten the atmosphere."

Jessica looked unconvinced.

"Which you should know, if you'd really studied psych," Steven pointed out.

"Oh, just shut up!" Jessica cried.

Steven began singing again. *"Oh, come ye, oh, come ye, to Be-eh-th-le-hem . . ."*

"Ready, Ms. Fowler?" The pilot of the Fowler-company jet turned around in his seat and smiled at her.

Lila was seated in one of the executive chairs right behind the cockpit. An open fashion magazine was in her lap, and a diet soda was on the little table next to her.

"Yes, yes, Captain. Let's get home."

Although she always drove back and forth between SVU and Sweet Valley, today when she'd gone back to her car in the parking lot, her battery had been dead. She'd called her mom, who arranged to have the car jump-started and driven back to Sweet Valley. Luckily, the company plane had been available.

As the jet's engines revved beneath her feet, Lila swallowed hard and deliberately turned the page of her magazine. Her nightmares had been silly. They had nothing to do with reality. She didn't believe in omens. She was sure it was perfectly safe to fly home.

Home. Where was home nowadays, anyway? Not Italy. She'd lived there only a couple months, and even with an Italian husband by her side, she had never felt at ease, or as if she fit in. When she'd come back to the U.S. after Tisiano's funeral, being back at her parents' house had been both comforting and weird. She'd been a married woman with her own house, her own marriage bed. To return to the room she'd slept in as a child, all white and ice-blue and ruffles, had been strange. But she loved having her parents near her again. She had had only a father for most of her life, and now she relished having a mother as well. She was looking forward to the holidays.

The jet's engines revved again, whining loudly even through the plush peach-colored carpeting. The ice in Lila's drink tinkled as the glass shook slightly on the table. Then they were rolling forward on the runway, and Lila rested her head back against the seat and held her glass.

As usual Captain Monroe took off effortlessly, easing the plane into the air so smoothly that it was impossible to tell when they'd left the ground. Lila glanced out the window. They were high above the town and swinging around in a huge curve to head home. She swallowed again. Everything was going to be fine. This was a piece of cake. There were no problems. After all, she didn't believe in omens.

Chapter
Nine

As Steven pulled the car into the far left lane of the highway, he glanced in the rearview mirror at Jessica, who was still looking thoughtfully out the window. Elizabeth had told him Jessica had a new romantic interest. He heartily approved. Things between him and Mike were definitely improving, but that didn't mean he wanted Jessica to be involved with Mike anymore. It was better that she move on with her life. She was still so young.

But he also knew he had to tell her about what had happened—with Mike, and the stove, and Mike's walking again. Billie already knew, of course. She'd picked him up from the hospital. But it wasn't fair for Jessica not to know. Besides, she was going to find out eventually, and it might as well be from him. She'd have a few weeks of vacation to get over the shock before classes began again.

Steven cleared his throat. "There's something

else we have to talk about. I mean, I have something to tell everybody."

The only sound in the car was the rattling and groaning of the Beetle's antique engine and the wind whistling through the gaps in the windows.

"Something happened to me a couple days ago," Steven began. "It had to do with Mike."

Jessica looked up. Steven saw in the mirror how his sister's eyes filled with worry at the mention of Mike's name.

Maybe it's not such a good idea right now. . . . But it's too late. . . .

"I was helping Mike with his rehab one night, like the judge ordered me to. He was in the living room, and we had dinner, and then I went into the kitchen to see about the dishes."

Steven glanced up at the mirror. Jessica's eyes were boring into the back of his head.

"I smelled gas but didn't think anything of it at first," he continued. Then he told them everything that had happened, from his losing consciousness, and Mike's throwing the doorstop through the window, to their trip to the hospital. "He saved my life," Steven said. "He risked his own life to save mine. If he hadn't thought to get fresh air in the room, we both could have died there."

Elizabeth's face was white, and she made a choking sound. "Why did you tell us before? Steven, are you OK?"

"I'm fine," he assured her. "I mean, the doctors said I probably shouldn't drive or operate heavy machinery. . . ." He glanced down at the steering wheel, pretending to be confused. "Uh-oh."

"That isn't funny," Elizabeth snapped. "You could have died—you *nearly* died, and you didn't even tell your own sisters!"

"I don't understand," Jessica said. "If you were passed out in the middle of the kitchen floor, how could Mike get the wheelchair past you to the window?"

"That's the other thing I had to tell you," Steven said, looking at Jessica in the rearview mirror. "Mike wasn't actually in his chair. He got to the kitchen on his own. I owe Mike my life because . . . he refused to sit there, to be paralyzed."

"What are you talking about?" Jessica said, gripping the back of the driver's seat, her face going as pale as Elizabeth's. "But Mike *is* paralyzed. The doctors . . . the bullet chipped his spine . . . everybody saw it, saw him in the wheelchair. I mean, Mike *can't* walk!"

"That's what I'm trying to tell you, Jess," Steven said. "That night when he saved my life, he realized that he was getting feeling back in his legs. He saw his doctor the next day, and they think his nerves are somehow regenerating. Apparently it happens in a small percentage of these spinal-injury cases. They hadn't mentioned it because they didn't think it would happen to him, and they didn't want to get his hopes up. But actually, Mike *can* walk now. Not great, but he's working on it. Probably in another month or two he'll be fine."

"I can't believe it," Jessica said, her voice trembling.

Elizabeth reached across Tom's lap and patted her sister's hand. Jessica eased back in her seat, as though trying to crumple herself into a tiny ball. Her eyes glazed over and she sat still, like a statue. In the mirror Steven couldn't tell whether his sister was afraid or relieved.

"You OK, Jess?" Steven asked.

Jessica only nodded. But he could see her eyes fill with tears.

Outside, the land was becoming more and more familiar. Steven had pulled off the highway and begun winding along the local roads through the town of Sweet Valley. Elizabeth held Tom's hand in hers, but as she passed all the landmarks, she could think of them only in terms of her past with Todd. The Dairi Burger, where they'd hung out with their friends all through high school. Sweet Valley High, where Todd had been the star of the basketball team.

Elizabeth fought the melancholy feelings about those happy and innocent times being gone forever. It wasn't fair, she thought. She had Tom; she was happy, she reminded herself. Her life had moved forward and changed for the better. But still, as they passed the homes of all the people she knew, and all the familiar street corners, feelings of nostalgia overwhelmed her, practically forcing her to feel sad.

Where was Todd? Where was Enid? They

used to be such a big part of her life.

Everyone in the small car was quiet as they pulled onto the Wakefields' street, Calico Drive. Everything looked the same, but for some reason Elizabeth thought everything should look different.

The big familiar house and the stretch of green lawn came into view. Suddenly Elizabeth felt Tom grip her hand harder, as if he knew she needed reminding of what was past and what was present. Elizabeth felt better, and she gave him a smile.

"You don't have to ring the bell, Liz," Jessica said, tapping her foot on the steps as Elizabeth and Tom hesitated at the door. "I mean, it *is* our house."

"It just doesn't *feel* like our house anymore," Elizabeth muttered, pressing the doorbell.

Jessica rolled her eyes and pushed past her twin.

"Jessica! Elizabeth!"

Alice Wakefield appeared in the doorway. She was wearing a bright-red cotton sweater with a large plaid appliqué bow, and a matching plaid kilt skirt. She looked very Christmassy. Her blond hair was sun-streaked, and her skin glowed with a deep Caribbean tan.

Wow, she looks great, Jessica marveled. *The best I've ever seen her.*

"Mom!" Elizabeth cried, rushing past Jessica. She flung herself into her mother's arms and hugged her tight.

Then it was Jessica's turn, and Steven's. Billie

and Tom stood there a little awkwardly.

"Mom, you remember Tom," Elizabeth said, pulling him closer.

"Of course," Mrs. Wakefield said with a welcoming smile. "It's good to see you again. I'm so glad you could join us for Christmas," she said. Then she turned to Billie and put an arm around her shoulder. "Billie, you look wonderful! I haven't seen you in ages."

Billie grinned.

"Where's Dad?" Elizabeth asked excitedly as they moved into the foyer and put down their bags.

"I sent him to the store for a few things," Mrs. Wakefield said.

"But his car's in the driveway," Steven said.

"I made him walk. During vacation he put on . . . well, let's just say he needs to exercise."

"How was your vacation?" Elizabeth asked eagerly. "You *look* like you had a great time."

"We *did*," Mrs. Wakefield said. "It was wonderful. I can't wait to tell you about it. And the food! You can't imagine. I must have gained ten pounds!"

"That's great, Mom," Elizabeth said, chuckling. "But I don't think you have to worry about your weight."

Mrs. Wakefield gave everyone a warm smile. "You all look so *good*. All grown up. All my babies grown up and gone off to college!"

"Mother!" Jessica moaned, rolling her eyes.

"But enough about me," Mrs. Wakefield said cheerfully. "Let's sit down in the family room and get caught up. I know we've talked on the phone a lot in the past week, but I want you to tell me everything again. How was your semester? Was it exciting?"

Jessica and Elizabeth exchanged nervous glances.

"You could say that," Steven said evenly.

"It was . . . everything we thought it would be," Tom threw in. "And more."

Elizabeth squeezed his arm in appreciation.

Maybe he'll actually pull it off, Jessica thought, looking at Tom.

"And how were your exams? Did you get all finished up?"

They all chorused yes.

"Jessica?" her mother asked. "What about you? How did your exams go?"

Jessica shrugged. "No problem."

Looking nonplussed, Mrs. Wakefield's forehead wrinkled with disbelief. "Really?"

Jessica forced an awkward smile. "Really."

Mrs. Wakefield's brow knitted. "Am I imagining things, or is my mother's intuition telling me that you're not giving me the whole picture?"

Steven quickly stepped forward and draped his arm around Jessica's shoulder. "She's just tired out from exams, Mom. Remember what I was like right after my first set of finals? It's always much harder than you expect."

Mrs. Wakefield almost looked convinced. "Well, here's something that will wake you up,

Jessica," she said. "A few minutes ago a nice young man called to wish you a merry Christmas. Here, I wrote down the message." Mrs. Wakefield handed her a piece of paper.

"James called?" Jessica asked, suddenly brightening.

"James? No, he said his name was . . ." Her mother looked down at the note. "That's it: Mike. He sounded darling, Jess."

Feeling shocked, Jessica clenched her jaw. Her hands shook as she unfolded the note.

Merry Christmas to the most beautiful woman I know. Your friend, Mike.

"He was so polite on the phone," Mrs. Wakefield continued. "He asked all about our vacation. He seemed to know everything—where we'd been, when we came back. He must be very special for you to tell him so much about us."

Jessica winced at the irony, but she bit her lip and nodded.

There was a long pause before Tom dutifully jumped in. "Dinner smells, uh, well, *done*," he said.

Everyone stifled their laughter.

"Yeah, what's for dinner, Mom?" Elizabeth asked, as if determined to change the subject.

"All the favorites. Jessica's Chinese chicken. Elizabeth's favorite side dish."

"Cold rice and vegetable salad?" Steven guessed.

"And your dad's favorite dessert."

"Peach cobbler! Yum. I can't wait," Elizabeth said.

"It'll be done in just a few minutes. Girls, why don't you get settled in upstairs? You'll be sharing Elizabeth's room. Billie and Tom, maybe you can help me in the kitchen. I want to hear everything about you two. Billie, maybe you can give Tom some advice on how to survive among the crazy Wakefields."

With Mike's message still gripped in her hand, Jessica watched her mother lead Billie and Tom away.

That was a close call. What was Mike doing, calling here like that? What would Mom do if she found out the truth about us? Hasn't he done enough damage?

With a shiver Jessica had a sudden inkling that she wouldn't have to wonder for long.

"Can I help you with the dishes or something, Mrs. Wakefield?" Tom asked.

"Aren't you sweet? I'll tell you what: While you tell me something about yourself, I'll hand you the dishes and you can stack them over there on the counter. We can sort out everything for the table in a minute."

"Sure thing."

Mrs. Wakefield handed over a stack of china plates, and Tom reached for it quickly. Too quickly. The stack wobbled, then rattled alarmingly. Tom juggled the whole thing with a loud clatter and finally set it safely down. Out of the corner of his eye, he could see Mrs. Wakefield throwing a glance his way.

Great, he thought. *Now she thinks I'm a total klutz.*

Tom looked out the window at the sky. It was dark. There were no stars, so he picked a wispy cloud and wished on that. *Please, just let me get through this holiday. Let everything go perfectly. Let Elizabeth's parents think I'm wonderful.*

Just then they all heard the front door slam.

"Dad!" Elizabeth cried from the living room, and ran out to greet her father.

Tom took a deep breath and wiped his hands on his pants legs. He had to make a good impression on Elizabeth's father. Smiling, Mrs. Wakefield handed him a stack of salad bowls and headed for the door to greet her husband. But just as she reached the door, it opened inward, surprising her.

"Oh!" She laughed, stepping back quickly. Right behind her, Tom leaped back out of her way. As he backpedaled to regain his balance, he tripped on the leg of a kitchen stool. Then he was falling in horrified slow motion, thinking only, *Oh, no.* A second later he heard the crash of seven china salad bowls shattering against the floor, sending shards everywhere.

When he opened his eyes again, he saw a crowd of Wakefields in the doorway, looking at him. They suddenly looked like an opposing team, like a crowd of linebackers he had to rush through to get into the end zone. Mrs. Wakefield looked sympathetic, Mr. Wakefield looked surprised, and Jessica and Steven were red from stifling their laughter. Tom flushed with humiliation.

That's it, he thought. *I've blown it. They'll never take me seriously now.*

"I'm so sorry, Tom," Mrs. Wakefield said, concern on her face. "That was all my fault. Are you all right? I hope you didn't cut yourself."

"I'm fine," Tom muttered. "But I broke all your dishes."

"Don't worry about it for a minute," Mrs. Wakefield commanded. "It's not a problem."

"I'll clean it up," Elizabeth offered.

"I'll help," Tom said meekly.

"Why don't we give them some room," Mr. Wakefield said. "Kids, join us in the living room when you're done."

"OK, Dad," Elizabeth said.

Everyone trooped out of the kitchen and the door swung shut behind them.

"It wasn't your fault," Elizabeth said again, getting out the broom and dustpan. "That could have happened to anyone."

Tom knelt with the dustpan while Elizabeth swept. "Yeah," he said dourly. "But why did it have to happen to *me, now, here?*"

Mike carefully took the chicken potpie out of the oven. He made sure the stove was off, and all the gas burners as well. Then, slowly and carefully, he carried the tray into the living room. Nowadays he was getting around with just a cane for support, although he'd noticed that when he was tired he tended to feel much weaker and more off balance. He'd been going to rehab every day at the hospital and religiously doing his exercises at home.

It had been nice to see Steven earlier. The doorstop was propping the kitchen door open already. Mike smiled when it caught his eye. He sat down on the couch and leaned over the coffee table to eat. He guessed that Steven and Jessica, and of course Elizabeth, were already home by now. Jessica had probably already gotten his telephone message. He wondered how she had reacted. Had she been pleased, or at least secretly pleased? Had Steven told her about his walking again? Did it even matter to her? He had to believe that it did. He had to have some hope.

Looking around the apartment, he saw once again how empty and barren it was, ever since that night Jessica had packed up and taken all her things. She was the one who had made the small apartment seem like a home. She'd brought light and life into it, made it a welcoming place to come home to. And he had destroyed it. His stupidity had turned it into a nightmare for her, for both of them.

The violent ending to it all flashed before him. The shouting. The deafening screams. The gunshot . . .

He blinked it all away.

"That's over," he murmured. "That's not me anymore. The Mike McAllery who got shot is dead."

Flicking the TV on with the remote, he channel-surfed through all the Christmas specials, all those happy families gathered around all those burning Yule logs, singing cheery carols. He thought of the Wakefield family sitting around the dining-room table. Mrs. Wakefield had sounded so nice on the phone. He'd thought about flying home to be with his own mother. Maybe he would call her to wish her a merry Christmas. Maybe she would call him. Then again, maybe not. That's the way it always seemed with them. Relatives in name only. The thought of flying out to see her lingered in his mind for about five seconds, then evaporated like smoke. His heart was tugging him somewhere else.

Bored, he flipped through the channels, searching for some distraction. He found the home-shopping network and watched some celebrity whose name he couldn't remember demonstrate a food processor. He was immediately reminded of Jessica. Once she'd moved in with him, she had been determined to learn how to cook. She'd asked him to get her a food processor. Their marriage had ended before he'd had a chance to buy her one.

The celebrity on the screen put the food processor away and held up a small black velvet box. She smiled knowingly at the unseen audience, peeked inside the box, then rotated it to the camera. Mike sighed when he saw what was inside: a glittering diamond ring.

"What are you waiting for, guys?" the celebrity dared the audience with a wink. "How could anyone resist a ring like this? What better way to tell your special someone, 'I love you and want

112

to spend the rest of my life with you'?"

Mike's eyes narrowed. *This time I could do it right. A proposal, a ring, everything the way it should be. Jessica couldn't say no to that.*

Reaching for a pen, he wrote down the phone number on the TV screen, then punched it into the phone.

Before the operator answered, he remembered that he had set Jessica free—and that she'd been happy to go. He dropped the phone back down. He had to let her go.

No. I can't. I won't. Not ever.

He thought of the message he'd left at the Wakefields' for Jessica. He would have given a lot to have seen her face when she'd received it.

"A merry-Christmas phone call is totally bogus," he said to himself, throwing down the remote. "A message just isn't good enough for her. If I'm going to do it, I have to do it right. In person. I have to at least *try.*"

The clock in the kitchen was ticking so loudly, he thought the sound was coming from inside his head. His fingers fell into its rhythm.

I can't just show up, he realized. *I have to call ahead. My days of crashing parties are over, and Jessica needs to know that.*

Mike picked up the phone and dialed the shopping-network number.

"I'd like to place a rush order," he said to the operator. "One diamond ring. Just like the one on the program. I need to have it by Christmas."

Chapter Ten

"Mom, that was fabulous," Steven said, leaning back from the table and patting his stomach.

"Now I know where Steven learned to cook," Billie said, smiling at him. "That was delicious, Mrs. Wakefield."

In her chair Jessica pretended to choke with surprise. She dramatically took a sip of water. "Steven? My brother, Steven, cook? Mr. Undomesticated? Mr. Barely Housebroken? You mean he actually knows what kitchen utensils are?" Her blue-green eyes stared at Billie uncomprehendingly.

Grinning, Elizabeth took Tom's hand under the table and squeezed it. He smiled too, apparently glad the spotlight was off him for once.

"Sure," Billie said, patting Steven's shoulder. "He's a good little cook."

Steven blushed as his family started laughing.

"He is," Billie insisted, only making matters worse.

Jessica hid her titters behind her hand, but she didn't hide them very well.

"OK, OK, let's leave the poor guy alone," Mrs. Wakefield said. "Why don't we have coffee and dessert in the family room, and we can show you slides of our cruise?"

Half an hour later Elizabeth sat on the floor in the family room, happily leaning against Tom, while her parents flashed slides on the white wall.

"Oh, look, this is the sundeck. It was so wonderful just to lie on the deck chairs with a good book while the cruise ship plowed through the ocean, taking us to another amazing port," Mrs. Wakefield said.

"Yeah. And be sure to notice your mother's good book," Mr. Wakefield said, standing up to point out the title on the slide image. It was clearly a thick, glossy romance, and everyone laughed.

"Well, the sun was too hot to really let your brain focus on anything heavy," Mrs. Wakefield said primly, clicking for another slide. "Look at that endless blue sky. It was so delicious."

They really deserved this vacation, Elizabeth thought, twining her fingers with Tom's. *But it's so strange to think that while they were lying on the sundeck soaking up the equatorial rays, we were at school, having such hard times.*

Her first several months at college had been miserable: Todd had dumped her, and she'd gained twenty pounds out of sorrow. Then Jessica had dumped her as a roommate, leaving her to live with her witch-from-hell roommate Celine Boudreaux . . . not to mention the horrible secret society that had literally tried to kill her. There had been a time when she'd been at the absolute lowest point of her life.

And Jessica. Her troubles could be summed up in one word: Mike. Images of police cars, Jessica crying hysterically, Steven handcuffed and jailed, flashed through her mind.

Steven's voice interrupted her reverie.

"I'm really glad you had such a great time, Mom," he said sincerely. "You and Dad deserve it. Now, I would just like to say how glad I am that you're back, and that we're all here together for the holidays, safe, healthy, and happy." He lifted his coffee cup in a toast.

"Hear, hear," Elizabeth said, lifting her own cup. *You don't know how close all of your children came to being none of those things.*

Out of the corner of her eye, Elizabeth saw her twin's face split in a forced, awkward grin. Jessica's eyes looked suspiciously shiny with unshed tears. A sharp pain stabbed Elizabeth's heart.

I don't know how much more of this she can take, Elizabeth thought, looking at her sister. Even on this beautiful, cozy evening, surrounded by people who loved her, the truth of the last month of their lives seemed to press against Jessica like an overflowing sea threatening to topple a dam. And not only Jessica. It seemed inevitable that sooner or

116

later one of them would do or say something that would send it all tumbling down on top of them, washing them away in a tidal wave of lies and dark secrets.

Standing up, Mrs. Wakefield started collecting dishes to take them into the kitchen. Tom stood up, holding his, and headed for the kitchen.

"Tom, watch—" Elizabeth began quickly, but it was too late. Her own plate had been on the floor, and her unfinished piece of chocolate cake had still been on it. Ever since she'd managed to get back into a size six, she'd been careful not to overdo the desserts. But in the darkness of the room Tom hadn't seen it. Now three chocolate footprints tracked across the cream-colored carpet of the family room.

Steven flicked on a lamp, and they all looked down at the rug. Tom looked completely horrified, and Elizabeth instantly felt sorry for him.

"It was my fault," she said immediately. "I never should have left my cake on the floor."

Mrs. Wakefield came back, and a tiny frown creased her forehead as she surveyed the damage. Then she glanced up at Tom and gave him a warm smile. Putting her arm around his shoulder, she said, "Tom, you look as though your best friend just died. Don't worry about it. This carpet resists stains. Remember, Steven used to live here."

Tom struggled to smile.

"Let me get some carpet cleaner and you'll see.

It'll be good as new." She headed back to the kitchen.

Elizabeth stood up and took Tom's hand to squeeze it. He looked as though he wished the earth would just swallow him up. "Don't worry about it," she whispered. "Don't even think about it." With a worried glance she saw that his face looked slightly green. "Besides," she whispered, "I'm grateful for the diversion." He nodded slightly, then stooped to take off his shoes. He headed to the kitchen to wash them off.

The phone rang, and Jessica ran to get it in her father's small study, just off the family room.

"So, Steven," Mr. Wakefield said, "how was the last month of school? Everything go OK? No problems while we were gone?"

Elizabeth could see Steven's eyes darting back and forth, desperately trying to think of an answer.

"Uh, Steven!" she interrupted. "Maybe you should take Tom upstairs and show him where all the blankets are and stuff. He's in the kitchen."

Steven was already out of his chair. "That's a great idea, Elizabeth." He pushed open the kitchen door, and they heard him talking to Tom.

Elizabeth was surprised that Steven had had a hard time thinking of something to say. She was suddenly worried about her brother. She'd thought he was the strongest of the three of them, but now she wasn't so sure. Would he be the one to break the code of silence?

Jessica's voice interrupted Elizabeth's thoughts.

118

"Hey, Liz!" she shouted from the study. "It's for you."

When they passed each other in the doorway, Jessica whispered at her, "And it's a *guy*!"

"For me?" Elizabeth asked, taken aback. Would Todd call her here? She went into the study and picked up the phone. "Hello?"

At first she couldn't hear anything.

"Hello?" she repeated. Then she could hear someone breathing on the other end.

"Who is this?" she demanded, annoyed. Then the blood drained from her face, leaving her pale. A dark voice, ugly, distorted, seeped through the phone. It said only three words: "I'm watching you."

Todd held the telephone receiver against his cheek for a few seconds, then hung it up. Pushing through the doors of the phone booth, he plunged back into the chilly night air of Sweet Valley. He retraced the same route he'd taken every night since he'd dropped out of SVU and come home: past Bill Chase's old house, then a right down the Wakefields' street, Calico Drive. Many of the trees and hedges on the front lawns were strung with winking Christmas lights. Here and there an illuminated plastic Santa urged on his reindeer from a neighbor's rooftop.

Then there were the Piedmonts. Mr. Piedmont was always sort of crazy, but you didn't know just how crazy until Christmastime. The day after

119

every Thanksgiving, he traced every window and doorway of his house with a string of bright white lights. A row of tall plastic candles glowed with electric light up each side of his walkway, looking more like missiles ready to be launched than candles. Then there was the fake snow on the rooftop, and the life-size Santa and reindeer. And few people could miss the huge inflated snowman on the front lawn, or the three-foot-wide red plastic ribbon that wrapped the house to end in a humongous bow over one window. Todd guessed Mr. Piedmont thought it made the house look like a large present. He was sure the Piedmonts used as much electricity during the holidays as the whole town did the rest of the year.

What a waste, he thought, moving on toward the Petrucellis'.

In front of the Petrucellis' driveway was an almost life-size crèche showing the birth of Jesus. A small make-believe stable was made of weathered wood, and the three wise men, bearing gifts, stood off to one side. Mary and Joseph flanked the small manger, filled with real straw. Something moved in the straw, and Todd's eyes widened. He paused for a moment and looked, then broke into a grin. The Petrucellis' cat, Muffin, had pushed out the plastic baby Jesus and was curled snugly in the manger, asleep. Snickering, Todd walked on. Even with Muffin in the manger, however, it was a pretty display, and certainly more in keeping with the season than the Piedmonts' tackiness.

Passing the Wakefields' house, Todd promised himself not to pause, not even to look. But from the corner of his eye, he saw Elizabeth's window. He'd memorized her room from all the times they had spent there together, studying, talking, kissing. He could picture the furniture, the desk, her bed. In his mind he traveled from her room into the hallway and down the steps to the family room, where they were all probably gathered around the fireplace, laughing, not thinking of him.

I should be there, he thought bitterly. He imagined himself sitting next to Elizabeth on the sofa, holding her hand, smelling the clean scent of her hair. Their knees would be touching, and he would be looking forward to later, when they could be alone.

But he wasn't there. He was outside, in the dark, in the street, walking by the house, where Watts was sitting next to Elizabeth, holding her hand, smelling her hair, looking forward to later when they could be alone.

Dejected and heartsick, Todd walked on.

He ended up where he had every night since he'd left SVU. In the old days, when he and Elizabeth had wanted to be alone, they'd often gone to Miller's Point. But that place depressed him now; it was full of high-school kids. Instead he went to the small nearby park. He and Elizabeth had spent a lot of time there last summer. They would sit beneath a huge tree and talk for hours, or simply lie on the grass and hold hands, content with the silence between them. Back then he'd thought they'd be together forever. He'd already been looking forward to their going away to college together. He'd already been anticipating that their relationship would progress, become more intimate.

And once we got to SVU, I ruined everything, Todd thought bitterly. *I forced the issue and lost Elizabeth forever.* There was a cold cement bench under their favorite tree, and he plunked himself down on it, feeling close to despair. He remembered the long hours they'd sat there, wrapped in each other's arms. He would kiss her, and she'd turn to him and whisper, "I love you, Todd."

Todd shook his head free of the picture.

"Not anymore," he muttered. "She doesn't love you anymore."

Someone giggled in the dark. A girl.

"Who's that?" a male voice called out.

"Who's *that*?" Todd demanded, suddenly on guard.

"Todd?"

Todd strained to see through the dark. He saw two figures untangling themselves from a close embrace.

Winston Egbert walked into the light of the nearby streetlamp. Even in the half dark, Todd could see his friend blushing.

"Who's that with you, Winston? . . . Oh, hi, Denise."

"Hi, Todd," Denise Waters replied, stepping

up beside Winston. Her hair was disheveled and had bits of leaves in it. Her face was flushed and happy, and she was zipping up her jacket.

"Hope I didn't interrupt anything," Todd said.

"Interrupt? You?" Winston said. "Why, what would you be interrupting?"

"Oh, Winnie," Denise said, taking Winston's hand. "Come on. You're not fooling anyone." She smiled at him affectionately.

I've got to hand it to him, Todd thought regretfully, looking at Denise. *Whoever would have thought that class clown Winston Egbert would have ended up with the smart and beautiful Denise Waters?*

"I didn't know you lived around here, Denise," Todd said.

"I don't. But Winston wanted me to spend some time with his parents."

"Oh, really," Todd said. *That serious already.*

"Yeah, since I can't make it to the reunion with him—" Denise began.

"I wanted her at least to see where I grew up," Winston finished her sentence.

"So are you taking Lauren to the reunion?" Denise asked Todd.

A stiff, plastic smile hardened on Todd's face.

Winston cleared his throat. "Uh, Denise— Todd and Lauren . . . uh . . ." He dragged an imaginary dagger across his throat.

"Oops, I didn't know," Denise said. "I'm sorry."

"Don't be," Todd replied casually. "I'm not. I'm taking . . . I mean, I'm going with Alexandra Rollins."

"Enid?" Winston asked in surprise.

"Neither of us had a date. We're old buddies. Why not?" Todd knew he sounded defensive.

"Oh, yeah, sure, why not?" Winston said. "That'll be fun. Alexandra's a great girl."

"Uh-huh," Todd said unenthusiastically.

"Hey, it'll be great to see everyone, won't it? And we'll be in the gym, where you had all those great games." He turned to Denise. "Todd was the basketball star of Sweet Valley High. No one could touch him."

"Yeah, well, that was then," Todd said.

As if sensing Todd's need to be alone, Winston and Denise awkwardly wished him good night, and Winston said he'd see him at the reunion. Todd barely nodded his acknowledgment.

At this time just last Christmas, he'd been playing against Sweet Valley High's rival, Big Mesa. It had been the best game of his life, and the most important. In his mind's eye he could see his own last-second shot at the hoop. It was in! Sweet Valley had won! They were the district champions, thanks to him. The cheerleaders had gone wild. His teammates had clapped him on the back. Coach had congratulated him. But best of all was Elizabeth, leaping out of the stands, running onto the court, and hugging him.

And look at this Christmas. Everyone's lives had

moved on. Lila had been married and widowed. Winston had started dating Denise. Bruce had inherited a million bucks. Jessica had married and then had her marriage annulled. And he had stupidly dumped Elizabeth and then lost his virginity to someone he didn't even care about. Since then he'd gotten suspended from the basketball team and dropped out of college.

What did the future hold for him?

Todd winced as he looked into the darkness of the trees. He imagined Elizabeth and Tom Watts sitting by a roaring fire in their house. Elizabeth was rocking a blond baby in her lap. Tom was sitting next to them, smiling at the baby, stroking Elizabeth's hair.

Then Todd saw himself living in some big city, a benchwarmer on a last-place semipro basketball team with a roster of over-the-hill scrubs with beer-bellies and tattoos. It was a cold city, maybe in the Northeast, or the Midwest. His apartment was cold, too, and was right above a sleazy bar frequented mostly by bikers.

For all his mistakes, sentenced to a life of loneliness.

He had to face it: He didn't have much of a future. Suddenly he shook himself out of his delirium and found himself standing alone in the dark.

"Yeah, see you at the reunion, Egbert. Looking forward to it," he said softly, knowing they'd been gone for a while. Then he turned and walked away into the darkness.

Chapter
Eleven

The lamp cast a warm glow in Mike's apartment. He glanced around, pleased at how clean the place looked. Yep, he was getting his act together. Things were going good. The first step had been the apartment. If he wanted Jessica to come back, he had to give her a nice place to come back to. And a nice guy to come back to as well.

Looking at his watch, Mike saw that it wasn't too late to call. He searched his wallet, then pulled out a small crumpled piece of paper. Before he could lose his nerve, he picked up the phone and dialed the number.

"Hello?"

Mike breathed a sigh of relief. It was Mrs. Wakefield again.

"Mrs. Wakefield? Maybe you'll remember me. My name is Mike McAllery. I left that message for Jessica with you yesterday."

"Oh, yes. Jessica was so excited to hear from you."

"She was?" Mike asked, surprised. "Is . . . is Jessica there, Mrs. Wakefield?"

"Well, she is, Mike. But can I have her call you back? She's kind of in the middle of something."

In the background Mike could hear uproarious laughter. The Wakefields sounded so happy together, so much like a real family. Together on the holidays, just like families on TV. Just the way it should be.

Then it struck him. For the first time in his life he had the desire for companionship. *Permanent* companionship. Not just a wife. He'd had that, as short-lived as it was. No, he wanted more. Children . . . home . . . *family*. He wanted it all. And he knew exactly whom he'd like to have that family with.

"Could I have her call you back in a little while, Mike?" Mrs. Wakefield asked.

"Actually," Mike began, "I was wondering if it would be OK for me to drop by on Christmas Day. I have to be in the area on business anyway, and I thought maybe I'd come by for a few minutes and see Jessica, if that's OK."

"Business?" Mrs. Wakefield asked. "So you're not a student?"

Mike was tongue-tied for a minute. "N-no, not exactly."

"But you live up near the university?"

"Yes, that's right," Mike replied.

"Well, I'm sure Jessica would love to see you

127

tomorrow, Mike. Why don't you hold on and I'll go and ask her."

Suddenly the thought came to him: His visit should be a surprise. If she was missing him, it would be the best Christmas present he could give her. And if she wasn't, he thought dejectedly, then at least he'd get in the door; at least he'd have the chance to convince her in person. She'd see for herself how different he was. He knew she still loved him. He just *knew* it.

"Wait, Mrs. Wakefield—I have an idea."

"Good night, darling," Mrs. Fowler said, enfolding Lila in a hug. "I'm so glad you're with us this Christmas."

Lila hugged her mother back, relishing the comfort. She knew her mom really meant, "We're glad you're with us instead of in Italy."

"I'm glad to be home too, Mom," she said, managing a smile.

"Now, do you have everything you need? I asked Susan to put out some extra towels for you."

"I'm fine, Mom. Everything's fine."

"Well, then, I'll see you in the morning." With a final kiss Mrs. Fowler headed back downstairs, where she and Lila's father were still attending to the details of his huge company Christmas party at Fowler Industries.

Still smiling, Lila went into her bathroom and brushed her teeth, then changed into her nightgown. She'd have to call Jessica tomorrow to see if she wanted to go to the mall for some last-minute shopping. She already had most of what she needed, but there were still a few little stocking stuffers that she wanted to get.

Climbing into her bed, Lila tried not to feel a twinge of apprehension. Lately it had been harder and harder to look forward to going to bed. Her nightmares hadn't gone away—in fact, if anything, they had increased.

It's just silliness, she told herself, pulling up her silk-covered down comforter. *It's just my subconscious trying to work through the tragedy of Tisiano's death.* In one of her women's magazines she'd read an article about how sometimes dreams served a purpose like that. It had made sense to her. *I'm just not going to think about it. I'm going to think about what courses I'm going to take next year, and about when I become a Theta, and how as soon as I'm a Theta I'm going to try to get Jessica back in, too.* . . . Nodding determinedly, Lila turned off her lamp and snuggled down into her covers.

"Elizabeth, where are you going?" Jessica whispered to her twin as Elizabeth started to climb out of bed. It was past midnight. The house had been dark and quiet for a long time. The twins were sharing Elizabeth's room so that Billie could have Jessica's room on the other side of their shared bathroom. The Wakefields had said apologetically that they knew Steven and Billie lived together, but that in their house they really couldn't condone their sharing a room unless they were married. Steven and Billie had said they understood. Tom was set up downstairs on the couch in the family room.

"I'm just going to the bathroom," Elizabeth whispered back.

Jessica clicked on the bedside lamp. Elizabeth blinked like a deer caught in the glare of headlights.

Even though they'd been home for just a few hours, it was easy to tell Jessica's side of the room from Elizabeth's. Jessica's already resembled an earthquake zone. There were two separate pyramids of clothes on the floor and a third on a chair; a duffel bag overflowing on the bureau; CDs scattered on the floor around her portable CD player.

In contrast, Elizabeth's side was as neat and uncluttered as it had been when they'd arrived. In fact, it looked a lot as it had when she'd left for college back in September: a rectangular table held her computer, printer, and a neat stack of computer paper; above it was a perfectly aligned shelf full of reference books and school supplies. Under the window stretched the chaise lounge she'd found for five dollars at a tag sale and had reupholstered in soft pale-blue velvet. It was where she'd done all her reading for high school, and where she'd started a new novel a few minutes before going to bed.

"You're going in the wrong direction," Jessica

130

pointed out with a smug grin. "The bathroom's that way, remember? Over *there*." She motioned to the door at the opposite end of the room.

"Uh, I'm thirsty. I'm going to get a glass of juice."

Jessica almost laughed at the guilty expression on Elizabeth's face. "Elizabeth, who do you think you're talking to? The most gullible person on the face of the earth? Please. This is Jessica, remember? I know you're going downstairs to visit Tom. You're so transparent. It's like you're made from Saran Wrap," Jessica said in mock disgust.

Elizabeth frowned at her. "I just want to go down and say good night. And make sure he has enough blankets and stuff."

"Oh, good idea," Jessica said with exaggerated approval. "You never know when the central heat will just suddenly go out completely."

Without deigning to answer, Elizabeth very quietly opened the hall door, then paused to listen for any sounds.

"Liz!" Jessica said in a loud whisper. Her sister looked around. "Try not to get caught." She smiled at Elizabeth understandingly.

Elizabeth smiled back, then was gone.

Still smiling, Jessica lay back down and clicked off the light. There was hope for Elizabeth, after all. Maybe Tom *was* good for her. Old Todd Yawn-a-Minute Wilkins would never have gotten her to sneak downstairs. However, for Elizabeth's sake, Jessica hoped her parents wouldn't find her with Tom. It would nip her daring streak right in the bud.

As Jessica lay in bed, she heard another door open and close down the hall. She frowned. Was it her folks? No. She pinpointed the sound as having come from Steven's room. Listening closely, she tracked footsteps down the hall.

Yep—it was Steven, heading into Jessica's room, where Billie was sleeping. Jessica's nose wrinkled as she thought about her own bed with them in it. Bleah.

Flopping over, she thought for a moment with amusement what it would be like if her parents found out what was going on. It would be fun to see her siblings get into trouble for once, especially since she herself was chastely alone in Elizabeth's room like a little Christmas angel. Punching her pillow, she rolled over and thought some more. In some ways Elizabeth was doing a very Jessica-like thing, and she was doing a very Elizabeth-like thing. She hoped it wasn't the beginning of a trend. She shook her head. Nah. She knew that if her boyfriend was in the house right now, she would sneak down to be with him. She just didn't happen to have anyone, that's all.

But that was going to change. *James*. Settling herself under the covers, she remembered how good-looking he was, how attentive he had been the night they'd gone to dinner. She hoped her life was starting a new chapter, and that James would be a major part of it.

*   *   *

I love this house, Tom thought dreamily as he lay in the darkness of the Wakefields' family room. The fold-out couch wasn't too bad, he decided. He pulled his sheet and blanket around himself, listening to the quietness of the house.

All the rooms even smell like Elizabeth. Walking around, I can smell her perfume. And it's a real family house, with togetherness and laughing, arguing and making up . . . A wave of sadness swept over him as he thought of everything he'd never have. He tried to picture the faces of his family— his parents, his older sister, his little brother. They had all died last year in a car accident on their way up to SVU to see him play football in the biggest game of the year. Until recently, he'd blamed himself.

He still thought of his family every day. No matter how much he'd tried to slow down, time kept passing, fading their images. It was getting harder and harder to remember what they looked like. All that remained was a gaping hole in his heart. Sometimes their absence was actually a physical ache.

But Elizabeth was helping him move on. Slowly but surely she was easing the pain. When he was with her, she made him feel alive again. Looking at her face, falling into those blue-green eyes, was like looking into his own future. And that future was bright. She was so alive, it was like being with life's energy itself. She was almost an addiction. He didn't think he'd ever be able to live without her.

He pictured her sleeping peacefully upstairs and smiled. One day, he hoped, he would be able to watch her sleeping beside him.

"Tom?" a soft voice whispered.

He sat up quickly. "Elizabeth?"

A dark shape moved forward, and then Elizabeth was caught in a shaft of moonlight. Outlined in the glow, she came toward him like an apparition, her blond hair luminous, her night-gown flowing behind her. She was too beautiful to be true. Tom's mouth went dry.

Tiptoeing across the carpet, she paused, then sat on the edge of the fold-out mattress. Tom reached out and ran his hand along her arm.

"Hi," he said softly. "I was just missing you."

"I was missing you, too," Elizabeth admitted. "Are you OK? Do you have everything you need?"

"I do now."

In the pale moonlight he thought he could see her smile. "I'm glad you're here," she said.

"Me too. Except I seem to be systematically destroying your parents' house."

Elizabeth laughed gently. "Don't worry about it. I'm sure they don't think anything about it." She crossed her arms and rubbed her hands against them.

"You cold?" Tom asked, his heart increasing its steady pounding.

She nodded.

Without a word he shifted his weight over and held up the edge of the covers. She hesitated. Although they had lain together on top of their beds at school, making out, they had never been under the covers together in their nightclothes.

After another minute of hesitation, Elizabeth crawled into bed with Tom. He felt as if he couldn't breathe. Her nightgown was chilly against his bare chest, and he could feel her small, icy feet against his.

"You're nice and warm," she said softly.

He shifted again so he could lie on his side holding her. "You'll be warm in a minute." He listened to her quiet breathing next to him and felt a fierce rush of happiness. "I'm glad you came down." Slowly, gently, his lips found Elizabeth's. Her mouth yielded under his, and he intensified the pressure. Their bodies were pressed together tightly, their arms holding each other strongly. It was their most passionate kiss ever, fueled by the relief of finishing their final exams and the distance they'd been forced to keep these last few days.

Pulling away, breathing hard, Elizabeth whispered, "I love you, Tom."

"I love you too." Stroking her hair, Tom kissed her mouth again, then trailed a fiery line of kisses down her neck. A tiny sound escaped her, and Tom thought he would go crazy.

"You're so beautiful," he said hoarsely, leaning back to see her in the dim light. "I can't believe how happy I am."

"You are?" Elizabeth whispered, turning toward him. "Promise?

"Promise." Tom kissed her again, then drew her close under the blankets. In the darkness it seemed as if nothing in the world could hurt them.

Well, almost nothing, Tom thought. "Elizabeth, I'm worried," he began softly. "I really wanted to make a good impression on your parents."

"You did," Elizabeth said, turning to him. "They really like you—I can tell. I'm sure they think you're nice, and funny, and smart . . ."

"And a total klutz." Tom flicked her nose lovingly.

Elizabeth laughed quietly. "I told you to quit thinking about it," she said. "All they care about is if we care about each other, and if you make me happy. And we do, and you do, and that's all there is to it." She kissed his neck and wrapped her arms around his chest.

Tom felt his throat closing with another rush of emotion. Silently, in the darkness, he took her in his arms again.

Chapter
Twelve

Steven slipped through the open door and tiptoed toward Jessica's bed.

"You don't fool anyone, Wakefield," Billie's voice whispered in the dark.

Once his eyes adjusted, Steven could see her sitting upright in bed, waiting for him. All he wanted to do was crawl into bed and hold her tightly in his arms. He wanted to forget about his family and Jessica's problems for a while.

Billie lifted up the covers for Steven to slide in, and he did. They faced each other and snuggled closely together, just as they did at home. Steven was so glad that they had worked out their problems, and that Billie had moved back a few days before. He knew they were both still recovering from the trauma of their breakup and Billie's moving out, but they were definitely making progress. Over the last week they'd spent hours talking everything out, and they had decided together that they wanted the relationship to last.

"Hmmm . . . this feels nice," Steven murmured.

"Yeah," Billie said softly. "It looks like we got through the first evening without anyone blurting out anything. Think we can keep it up?"

Steven sighed and buried his face against her shoulder. "I don't know," he admitted. "It's harder than I thought it would be, and I thought it would be a total bitch. I'm a terrible liar."

"I know," Billie agreed.

"I feel like a criminal around my parents, like I've lied to them. Important stuff happened these last few weeks. Important, life-changing stuff. And we can't tell my parents about it. I think that's wrong, no matter what I told Jessica."

Billie nodded understandingly. "But we promised Jessica—"

"I know," Steven groaned. "But I think she should confide in my parents. She *needs* them. Maybe they could help her somehow."

"Earlier today you said that it would be better for them not to know," Billie reminded him. "You thought your parents wouldn't be able to handle it. What's made you change your mind?"

"I don't know," Steven admitted. "They seemed so relaxed and happy tonight. We seemed so close as a family. And it's Christmas."

"You mean you're hoping that the spirit of forgiveness kicks in?" Billie said.

"I just think maybe they'd be more flexible and supportive than we thought," Steven said. "They

138

were in such a good mood. And Mom was so nice to Tom when he broke the dishes and tracked the chocolate cake all over the rug."

Billie laughed softly in the darkness.

"I just feel like maybe they've loosened up a bit," Steven added.

"Maybe they have," Billie agreed. "But I also know that you don't like having a secret. You're starting to feel guilty about it and want to come clean. But you're not the only one involved, Steven."

"I know. I don't want to hurt Jessica," Steven said. "But I don't want to hurt my parents, either. If they find out later that we've all been lying to them all this time, they'd be really disappointed. Also, lots of people must already know in Sweet Valley. People who are going to talk to my parents. There's no way it can stay a secret for much longer. I can't believe they don't know already."

Billie turned to him. Even in the dark he could see her worried expression.

"In the end, what's really worse?" he asked her. "Pretending nothing ever happened, or letting out the truth?"

In Elizabeth's room Jessica moved restlessly in her sleep. A fine sheen of sweat broke out on her forehead, and she mumbled something. Then she smiled, and her actions stilled.

James had come to spend the holidays with them. Thoughtfully, he had brought a heap of beautifully

139

wrapped gifts, one for every member of the family, and piled them with the others below the Christmas tree. He ate dinner with the family and charmed everyone. He was perfect, and after dessert her parents told her how proud they were of her. Afterward Jessica had made a bed for him on the family-room couch. As she kissed him softly on the cheek good night, James said: "I'll see you in the morning."

Jessica grinned mischievously. "If you're lucky, you'll see me before that," she whispered in his ear, then went to bed herself.

But she didn't fall asleep. She waited until she was sure everyone was sleeping, then rose and went quietly downstairs. There was a dark form on the couch, rising and falling gently in sleep. Jessica tiptoed over and sat on the bed.

His back was broad and warm, and Jessica gently placed her hand against it. She would wake him up, and they could talk softly in the darkness. Before she woke him, she looked admiringly at his figure. He had wide shoulders and a narrow waist. Then the blanket went flat. She stared. He had no legs! Frantically she shook his shoulder. The sleeping form turned over and looked at her with a smile.

She opened her mouth to scream, but nothing came out.

It wasn't James. It was Mike! And his smiling face was awash in blood.

"Oh!" Jessica sat bolt upright, breathing hard. Her nightgown was damp with sweat. Quickly she looked around the room, as if afraid of what she'd see.

Then her muscles relaxed slightly, and she tried to control her breathing. She was in Elizabeth's room. She looked beside her—Elizabeth wasn't there.

It was just a dream, she told herself. *Just a dream.* Then she remembered James. There *was* a James. He wasn't a dream. He'd be picking her up in his red Miata in three days.

"James," she said aloud. But her eyes clouded. It wasn't James she was remembering. It was Mike. Still Mike. Always Mike.

Will I ever get him out of my life? she wondered.

Jessica could imagine him standing beside her. She could practically smell him. She used to love the way they looked together, her the perfect southern-California girl, and him, wild, dark, unbearably handsome. Only a month ago nothing excited her more than riding the back of his motorcycle, hugging him around the waist as they roared along the ocean roads with the wind blowing through her hair. She'd thought they were a walking advertisement for living on the edge.

And then it all ended. One argument too many, one threat too far, one gunshot.

She felt a tug of sadness in her heart. "Where is he now?" she whispered. "What is he doing?"

"I meant to tell you," Elizabeth said sleepily. "I had a weird phone call earlier." A few weeks earlier Elizabeth had had several threatening phone calls. They had really disturbed her, especially since she knew that William White had been locked up in a psychiatric hospital. She'd never been able to figure out who was calling her, and in the end had decided to not think about it.

"That's right—I forgot to ask you who called." Tom nestled closer to her. "How was it weird?"

Despite the warmth of being in Tom's arms, Elizabeth shivered. "It was—threatening," she admitted. "This awful, eerie voice said, 'I'm watching you.'"

In the darkness Tom frowned and pulled back a bit to see her face. "Male or female?" he asked tersely.

Elizabeth thought back. "Male, I think."

"Goddammit," Tom swore, sitting up on his elbows. Elizabeth stared at him.

"What?" she asked.

"It was Wilkins," Tom said. "It had to be Wilkins."

Frowning, Elizabeth tried to remember the voice. "It didn't sound like him," she said. "But the voice was pretty distorted." Then she shook her head firmly. "No, Tom, this voice was scary, threatening. Todd might miss me and really want me back, but he would never threaten me. I don't believe it."

"Then who could it be?" Tom argued. "White's still nailed down at the loony bin."

Suddenly the light in the kitchen went on, flooding the family room with light.

With a quick gasp Elizabeth rolled off the sofa bed and underneath it, pulling in her legs just as her father appeared in the doorway.

So this is what a heart attack feels like, Tom thought hysterically, feeling as though his heart were pounding in his throat, choking him.

"Hope I didn't wake you, Tom," Mr. Wakefield said in a loud whisper. "But I thought I heard voices in here. Thought maybe we'd left the stereo on."

"Uh, no," Tom choked out unevenly. *That was just Elizabeth, in bed with me.* "I guess I was just muttering to myself," he said, desperately trying to sound cheerful and unconcerned. "You know, just working things out in my mind." He hoped with all his might that Elizabeth's nightgown wasn't peeking out from beneath the couch.

Mr. Wakefield smiled warmly. "I know how it is. Sometimes it's hard being in a strange house, trying to fall asleep. But I have the cure."

"You do?" Tom warbled.

"Yep. What you need is a midnight snack. Come on in here and we'll see what we can rustle up." Mr. Wakefield gestured toward the kitchen.

"Oh, no, that's OK," Tom stammered. "I'm not really hungry."

"Of course you are. You just don't realize it," Mr. Wakefield said firmly. "Now, how about a nice piece of chocolate cake? I insist."

There was nothing Tom could do. Elizabeth's father was waiting for him. Slowly he got out of bed, then pulled on a T-shirt. Excruciatingly aware of Elizabeth curled into a little ball on the cold floor beneath his bed, he left the room and followed Mr. Wakefield into the kitchen. *I'm sorry,*

Elizabeth, he thought sadly. *You know if I had a choice I would choose you over chocolate cake anytime.*

Streaks of golden-yellow sunlight flooded Elizabeth's bedroom. Jessica squirmed, her eyes still shut. She felt crowded, as though she could hardly move. And it was very hot. She tried to resist waking up, but it was no use. Rolling onto her other side, her feet hit something in bed with her. Other feet. Her eyes popped wide open, and she immediately relaxed.

So Ms. Goody Two-Shoes actually made it back to bed last night, Jessica thought gleefully, looking at her sleeping sister. She would have fun teasing Elizabeth about it today. Smiling, she pictured Elizabeth and Tom squirming at the breakfast table as Jessica dropped double entendres in front of their parents.

A scent wafted toward her gently, and Jessica sniffed. Elizabeth's room always smelled so fresh, Jessica mused. It must be her shampoo or something. Then she turned in bed, stretching. Her eyes widened again.

Jessica sat up and gasped.

A massive bouquet of peach-colored roses stood in a large glass vase on the night table.

"Gorgeous," Jessica whispered. "Expensive." Surely Tom Terrific hadn't sprung for these babies, had he? He'd never have the nerve to sneak them into the bedroom. Jessica spotted a small greeting card, a little island of white in the sea of flowers. She suddenly had a happy thought. "James!"

They must have been delivered this morning. Jessica leaped out of bed and buried her face in the flowers. Heavenly. She grabbed for the card and tore it open.

I miss you. . . .
Mike

Jessica swallowed hard and sat back on the bed.

"Mike," she whispered. Her hands started to shake. She looked at the huge arrangement of roses blooming in the room, filling the air with their sweet, heady scent.

What is he up to?

Frowning, she remembered Steven's news. Mike was walking. He seemed different. Changed.

"Hmm, morning," a sleepy voice said in back of her. Turning, Jessica saw Elizabeth slowly opening her eyes and stretching. When Elizabeth saw the flowers, she smiled.

"Are those for me?" she asked excitedly.

"I wish they were," Jessica said grumpily. "But they're for me, from Mike."

Elizabeth's mouth made a little O.

"Yeah," Jessica said bitterly. "That's how I feel, too." Suddenly feeling close tears, she burst out, "Oh, Elizabeth, what am I going to do? I left him; our marriage was annulled. It's over. Why won't he let me be?"

Sitting up, Elizabeth put her arms around Jessica. "I'm so sorry, Jess," she whispered. "I know how hard you're trying to get on with your life. You don't deserve to suffer like this. Maybe we should have Steven talk to Mike."

Jessica wiped her eyes and looked at the floor. "Mike's head is like a big rock. It wouldn't do any good. No, I'll just have to deal with him myself." She sniffled. "I mean, I don't hate him, even after everything that's happened. I don't think I could ever hate him. When we were first together, I was so happy. Maybe a part of me will always love him. But I've realized that this isn't a good time for us to be together." She turned tearful eyes to Elizabeth. "Do you believe that could happen? That we're maybe meant for each other, but just not meant to be together now?"

Elizabeth hesitated, then said, "Maybe. What are you going to tell him? Do you think the flowers are his way of apologizing?"

Jessica got out of bed, picked her robe up from the floor, and pulled it on. "Who knows?" she said doubtfully. "I'll just have to play it by ear until I talk to him and find out what's going on."

Downstairs, everyone except the twins was already around the kitchen table, dressed and eating.

"Well!" Mrs. Wakefield said cheerfully when Jessica walked in. "This has to be a first—Jessica beating Elizabeth to breakfast."

Moments later Elizabeth, in her robe, shuf-

146

fled in, trying not to meet Tom's eyes.

Jessica plopped into her chair and reached for the coffee.

"What about the forest that arrived for you this morning?" Mrs. Wakefield asked.

"What about them?" Jessica mumbled, taking a muffin from the basket.

Her father looked at her. "I thought they were beautiful," he said. "Someone went to a lot of trouble."

Jessica took a bite of muffin. "Yeah, they're nice," she said unenthusiastically. She looked up at Steven, but he frowned slightly and looked away. *He looks guilty,* Jessica thought. *He's got to keep it together.*

Apparently deciding to drop the subject, Mrs. Wakefield said, "What are everyone's plans today? Your dad and I have some errands to run, but someone can use my car if you need it."

"I think Tom and I are going to the mall," Elizabeth said, blushing a little. "Jessica, do you want to come? Or maybe Steven and Billie?"

Jessica shook her head but gave Elizabeth a grateful look. "I'm going to call Lila and see if she wants to do something. Thanks anyway."

"Billie and I are going to take an extended tour of Sweet Valley," Steven said. He put down his coffee cup. "Ready, babe?" Everyone smiled as Billie rolled her eyes and said, "Ready, dude."

They stood up and went to get their jackets. A minute later the front door slammed.

Soon Elizabeth stood up. "I better go get dressed. Tom, you can use Steven's shower upstairs if you want."

"Thanks." Tom put his napkin down, and they headed upstairs. Jessica frowned. She'd been so preoccupied, she'd forgotten to give them a hard time. Well, she'd do it later.

"OK, we'll see you in a couple hours, sweetheart," Mr. Wakefield said, leaving the kitchen.

"Later," Jessica said.

On her way out Mrs. Wakefield bent and whispered into Jessica's ear: "Are you OK? Mike seemed like a nice boy. He was so polite. And he's romantic, too, isn't he?"

If you only knew, Jessica thought, smiling grimly to herself. Then her mother left and Jessica was alone, thank heavens. She poured herself another cup of coffee.

She was still at the kitchen table, her head propped on her hands as she read the comics, when Elizabeth and Tom came downstairs.

"All fresh and pretty?" Jessica teased. Then she frowned, as though an idea had suddenly occurred to her. "You guys didn't shower *together,* did you?" she demanded, looking shocked.

"Shh!" Elizabeth hissed, hitting Jessica with a rolled-up piece of newspaper. Tom laughed.

"So how was last night?" Jessica prompted them. "You didn't get caught?"

"No," Tom said sourly. "But I never want to see chocolate cake again."

Laughing, Elizabeth took his arm, grabbed her mother's car keys, and pulled him outside.

What the heck did he mean by that? Were they getting kinky with chocolate cake? Jessica shook her head. *What am I thinking? This is Elizabeth we're taking about.* She resolved to pump her sister for details later.

When the phone rang, Jessica dropped her coffee cup into its saucer. "Please don't let it be Mike. Please don't let it be Mike," she murmured, reaching for the phone.

"Hello?" she asked weakly.

"Hello. May I speak to Jessica, please?"

Definitely not Mike.

"This is she."

"Hi, Jessica. This is James Montgomery."

"James!" Relief flooded through her.

"Yeah. I just wanted to see what time I should pick you up for the reunion. I'm really looking forward to it."

"So am I." Smiling, Jessica sat back down at the table, pulling the phone cord closer. As she and James talked about their plans, Jessica spotted Mike's card lying by her place mat. She picked it up, crumpled it into a ball, and threw it across the room into the garbage.

Mike? Jessica thought, listening to James's polite baritone. *Who's Mike?*

Chapter
Thirteen

"Oops, careful," Alexandra exclaimed, leaning against Todd. "These mothers with baby strollers are totally deadly." She took his arm and pressed closer to him as they walked.

Todd just shrugged. He'd called Alexandra the night before for lack of anything better to do, and when she'd suggested going shopping, he hadn't been able to come up with an excuse. At first it had been strange and awkward between them, as they recalled what had happened the last time they'd seen each other, but soon they had been able to relax a bit. After all, they were old friends; they'd known each other for years. And Alexandra didn't seem to be making any demands on him, for which he was grateful. In fact, he was glad to have someone to hang around with, since he felt as if none of his other old friends really wanted to see him.

Poor Todd. He's really having a hard time, Alexandra thought sympathetically. *But he's with me now. I have to try to help him.* She knew he was trying to be friendly and interested, but it was all too clear what was really on his mind. Alexandra resolved to try to cheer him up.

Slowly they pushed their way through the thick crowds. Alexandra still needed some small last-minute things, and she kept her eyes glued to the store windows, searching for inspiration. She was very conscious of Todd's body pressed against hers as they made their way through the throng. The mall was packed with shoppers who also had to finish their last-minute gift buying. Little kids were running wild, gleefully separated from their parents, teenagers were hanging out, trying to look cool, everywhere was the hustle and bustle of holiday insanity.

In the middle of the mall a Santa's workshop had been set up, and there was an incredibly long line of kids waiting to have their pictures taken.

Alexandra nudged Todd's arm. "Want to have your picture taken?" she teased. "You could make a wish."

Todd couldn't help smiling. "Yeah. Maybe I could ask Santa for my career back."

Tugging on his hand, Alexandra pulled Todd over to an electronics store. Maybe she could find something for her dad in there. "Todd, you know if there's anything I can do, all you have to do is ask," Alexandra told him seriously as they went in.

Todd nodded. "Thanks, Alex. But I think I need to dig myself out of this hole alone, you know?"

"OK." Alexandra bought her father an electric razor and got her cousin a Swiss army knife. Then they plunged out into the crowd again.

"Are you hungry?" Todd asked. "You want to get a piece of pizza?"

"Sure. I'll grab a table if you'll get in line."

Todd nodded.

What am I going to do with him? He's so down. I wish he'd just fall in love with me. Alexandra smiled to herself. *Not really. I'm not in love with him, either. But I wish I could help somehow.* She couldn't help thinking that if he were with Elizabeth, he'd feel better. Well, Alexandra could do everything that Elizabeth could, right? And even some things that she couldn't.

Soon Todd returned with two pieces of pepperoni pizza and two sodas on a tray. He sat across from her and took a bite.

"So have you finished all your shopping?" Alexandra asked him.

He nodded ruefully. "Since I left school, I've kind of had time on my hands. It's the first time in my life I had all my presents bought and wrapped before Christmas."

Alexandra grinned at him. "It's nice to know you've been using your time wisely. So what are you going to wear to the reunion?"

He shrugged, taking another bite of pizza. "I don't know. Maybe a pair of jeans and a T-shirt. Inside out." His eyes sparkled a little bit at her across the table.

She laughed quickly, embarrassed, then tossed a wadded-up napkin at him. "We agreed not to mention that again."

"Sorry. What are you going to wear?"

"I thought maybe a floaty baby-doll dress over a black unitard." She'd seen a cute dress in a shop window. Maybe she should backtrack and get it.

"That sounds nice," Todd said diplomatically. Alexandra laughed, because she doubted he had any idea what kinds of clothing she'd just described. But at least he was trying.

They ate silently for a few minutes, each lost in thought but taking some small comfort from the other's presence.

Alexandra remembered last year's Christmas. She'd spent part of the day with Todd then, too. But of course he'd been with Elizabeth, and they'd all been with the Wakefields. They had sung carols around the piano. Elizabeth had smiled radiantly as they fantasized about what college would be like. They had planned on being roommates, and Alexandra had sworn to find herself a gorgeous hunk so she could double-date with Elizabeth and Todd.

Sometimes I really miss her, she thought, blinking away a few sudden tears. *But here I am sitting with her ex-boyfriend, going to the reunion with him. Will she mind? Will it drive us further apart?*

Guiltily, Alexandra remembered that she'd been the one who'd broken away from Elizabeth, not the other way around. She was the one who

153

hadn't needed her best friend anymore. Once she'd changed her name from Enid to Alexandra, and her image from geeky to cool and sophisticated, and started to date Mark Gathers, she'd never looked back.

Until now. Lately she'd been looking back so often, she was beginning to feel as if she had whiplash.

Blaming her because Mark left me was wrong too, Alexandra admitted, taking a sip of her soda. *It's not fair to blame her for everything that's going wrong in my life. It isn't her fault. I can see that now.*

"Hey," Todd said gently. "Earth to Alexandra." He took her hand on top of the table.

"Sorry," Alexandra said, flustered, liking the feel of his touch far too much. "Just thinking. Ready to shop till we drop?"

Todd groaned, but he was smiling. "Ready as I'll ever be. Which isn't saying much."

"Come on, then." Alexandra got up and pulled him up with her, feeling just a little better than she had earlier that morning. Then, bravely, they faced the crush of people.

"I feel like we're refugees fleeing some invasion with all our belongings." Elizabeth laughed as she and Tom navigated through the mayhem at the mall with two big plastic shopping bags in each hand.

"I feel like a . . . umph! . . . a bumper car," Tom said, grimacing as the fifth unseen elbow in the last hour nailed him in the ribs.

"I keep forgetting what hard work Christmas is," Elizabeth admitted.

"We're programmed that way. A week after Christmas, you forget all the pain and the annoyance. If everyone remembered, no one would ever go shopping again."

"Until the credit-card bills start flooding in," Elizabeth joked, laying her head gently on Tom's shoulder.

Tom didn't have a free hand to put around her waist, so Elizabeth had to make do with a kiss on her cheek.

"Umph!" Tom moaned, taking a blow to the stomach. "Hey, watch it!" He and Elizabeth whirled around, but all they saw was a faceless mass of people. The culprit was gone.

"Look at that!" Elizabeth said excitedly.

"What? Where?" Tom twisted around clumsily.

"There! In the window of the men's store. For my father. What do you think?"

Elizabeth pressed her nose against the display window at dozens of ties hanging off a plastic Christmas tree.

"A tie?" Tom cried, aghast. "You want to buy a tie for your father? For *Christmas*?"

"Why not?" Elizabeth asked innocently. "I—I sort of always buy him a tie."

Tom rolled his eyes. "That's the point! Whenever a woman doesn't know what to get a man, she gets him a tie. It's about as much a surprise as the sun

155

coming up in the morning. A guy needs only so many ties."

"But men do need lots of ties," Elizabeth said. "Especially fathers."

"But *anybody* can buy your father a tie! Your father's *secretary* can buy your father a tie. You're his *daughter,* Elizabeth. Get him something that'll show him how much you love him."

Elizabeth gazed up at Tom adoringly. He looked so earnest, so *bothered*. It was adorable. But she also knew where his reaction was coming from. She knew he was really talking about *his* father.

I wonder how many times he's seen something he's wanted to give him, she thought. *I wonder how many times he's bought presents for his whole family in his mind but knew he'd never be able to get them anything again.*

She tried to picture his parents, brother, and sister, but she couldn't. And she knew she never would.

"OK, you win," she said. "Something meaningful. But *what?*"

"Follow me," Tom said, his face set with determination. He pushed off into the sea of shoppers like a boat shoving off from a dock. Head down, he forced his way through, Elizabeth trailing in his wake.

Finally they found what they were looking for, and they both realized it at once. They looked up at the entrance to Books 'n' Things and nodded to each other.

"I know, I'll get him *Their Eyes Were Watching*

God," Elizabeth said. "I loved that book so much. Now he can read it, and we can talk about it afterward."

"Exactly," Tom said, satisfied.

They surged toward the door, then ran smack into the back of a young couple.

"Hey, watch it!" Tom cried.

"You watch it!" the guy replied, whirling around.

Elizabeth almost dropped her bags in surprise. She flushed. "Oh, hi, Todd. Sorry." Then she noticed the girl with him. "Oh, hi, Alexandra." She must sound like a tape recorder, she realized. But she didn't know what to say. Todd and Alexandra had been holding hands. She plastered a smile on her face. "Doing some last-minute shopping?"

Alexandra forced a laugh. "Yeah. It was a terrible idea. I feel like . . . a piece of krill."

Elizabeth gave a spontaneous, sincere laugh. She'd always loved Enid's—Alexandra's—sense of humor.

"I know what you mean." She tried not to notice as Todd dropped Alexandra's hand casually. *Are they a couple? How weird.*

For a few awkward moments the four of them stood there, an island of stillness and silence in the fast current of screaming toddlers and harried parents and pacing Santas tolling their little tin bells.

Alexandra's eyes brightened. "Remember last year when the three of us practically begged people to let us into their stores when they were closing on Christmas Eve?"

157

Elizabeth smiled, then realized that Tom was looking distinctly irritated. "Yeah. That was wild. At least I'm doing a little better this year." *They're so far away,* she thought, looking at Alexandra and Todd. *I used to be closer to them than anyone on earth, except Jessica. Now they're apparently together, I'm with Tom, and we're all barely speaking to each other.*

"Well, I sure am looking forward to the reunion," Elizabeth said, trying to sound cheerful. But it came out sounding flat and fake, as if the reunion were the last thing on earth she wanted to do. And, right now, it was.

"Yeah, well, maybe you'll save me a dance," Todd said evenly, not looking at her.

Out of the corner of her eye Elizabeth could see Tom seething with anger. His jaw was clenched. His hostility toward Todd was so obvious that Elizabeth felt as if she were standing next to an angry dog. Todd, looking at Tom, didn't seem much better. She knew he hated Tom.

"Well, see you," Todd said finally. Taking Alexandra's hand again, he turned and headed into the crowd. Alexandra gave Elizabeth a forced, perplexed smile, then followed Todd.

Last year on Christmas Eve with Alexandra and Todd, she had been so happy, Elizabeth thought sadly. They had all been so happy then. Their futures had been so promising.

She looked up at Tom, but Tom was still staring angrily after Todd. She *was* happier, wasn't she?

Suddenly she had no idea.

*   *   *

"I'm glad we could get together," Jessica said to Lila as they rode the escalator toward the top floor of the mall. "It's nice to be chauffeured around in your Triumph again. Now we need to find totally hot dresses to wear to the reunion."

Lila smiled at her. "I thought you needed to buy presents."

"Oh, right, right," Jessica agreed easily. "We'll get to that. But first, the reunion . . . We have to look *devastating*."

"Sexy," Lila added. "More than sexy. Drop-dead gorgeous!"

"That's the spirit, Lila," Jessica said happily. It was just like old times. Shopping with Lila and her limitless credit cards was always good to cheer her up. Anything to take Mike off her mind for even a minute.

Jessica squeezed Lila's arm. "It's fabulous to have you back home. College'll be so much more fun with you around."

"Yeah. Next semester's going to be great," Lila agreed. "It'll be nice to be just a college freshman for a change." A shadow of sorrow flitted across her face; then it was gone. "Hey, isn't that Elizabeth?" she asked, pointing over the railing to the floor below.

Jessica peered over.

"It sure is," she said, laughing. "And naturally Tom Terrific is surgically attached to her—wait'll I tell you about last night. But . . .

159

uh-oh. Do you see who they're talking to?"

Lila leaned over the railing. "Alexandra and the Toddster!" She covered her mouth with her hands. "Oops. Are they holding hands?"

"It certainly looks that way to me," Jessica said primly. "Well. That must be a pretty interesting little meeting. Wish we could hear what's going on."

Laughing, they turned toward the clothes boutiques on the upper level.

"Yo, Fowler; Wakefield," a smooth male voice said behind them.

Lila's and Jessica's eyes met. "Bruce," they said at the same time. With identical weary sighs, they turned to face him. No way out of it.

"Patman," Jessica said casually, mimicking him.

His blue eyes narrowed a bit; then he smiled wolfishly. "So what are you two ladies doing here?" He slapped a hand to his forehead. "Oh, I forgot. It's a *mall.*"

Jessica rolled her eyes. "Do you need something, Bruce?" she asked pointedly.

"Yeah, but you said no, babe, remember?" He leered at her.

"OK, we have to go. Good seeing you, Patman," Jessica said coldly.

"Hey, hang on a minute," Bruce said. "Where's your Christmas spirit?"

"It's right here in this store. I have to go get it now," Lila said snidely. She just couldn't believe that this was the guy Alison Quinn was so hung up on. What could Alison possibly see in him?

160

Bruce laughed. "You guys going to the reunion?"

Reluctantly they nodded, wondering what kind of ammunition they were giving him.

"Then I guess I'll see you there," he said, flashing his famous smile.

Lila and Jessica turned to go without replying but were called back once more.

"Oh, Lila," Bruce said. "I meant to ask you—how's your flying doing?"

Lila frowned. "Why do you want to know?"

"Well," he began, "I still can't believe that you're the fancy pilot you say you are. I'd like to offer you the chance to prove it to me."

Lila bit her lower lip. "How?"

"Lila, you're not going to fall for this, are you?" Jessica whispered.

"Why don't you fly back to SVU with me after Christmas. I need to get back in time for the New Year's party. Once we're up in the air, I'll let you take the controls," Bruce said, watching her face. "Then we'll see once and for all if you're as good as you think."

Lila glared at him. On any other day she'd be happy to wipe that knowing smirk off his handsome face. But today, after all the nightmares she'd been having, she just didn't know if she was going to fly again anytime soon.

"Bawk, bawk bawk bawk," Bruce crowed softly.

"I'm *not* chicken!" Lila snapped. "I'm just really busy!"

"Yeah, right." Bruce laughed and began walking backward down the corridor. "If you change your mind, *chicken*, I'll see you at the flight field at eight o'clock on New Year's Eve. If you don't show, I'll know you were lying." He grinned and turned around, leaving the girls seething behind him.

"I can't think of a worse person to have inherited a million-dollar trust fund," Jessica said once they were safely inside Lisette's, their favorite boutique.

"Yeah," Lila agreed. "If his grandfather wanted to leave money to an animal, he should have just donated it to the World Wildlife Fund."

They wandered over to the dress racks.

"The pretty nice and kind of expensive things are over there," Lila said, pointing. "But over *there* are the incredibly hot and totally expensive dresses."

"What are we waiting for?" Jessica asked, marching over to the totally expensive rack.

Chapter
Fourteen

Elizabeth woke early on Christmas Day. When she was little, she'd always woken spontaneously at dawn on Christmas, too excited to sleep. *Looks like some things never change,* she thought giddily. For a moment she looked at Jessica sleeping next to her. Her sister's face was expressionless, poised in sleep. Elizabeth hated to wake her; she knew as soon as she did, that guarded look would come into Jessica's eyes. That look that said she'd been hurt badly and wasn't over it. The look that said she had secrets she'd never tell anyone. Elizabeth couldn't believe her parents hadn't seen that in Jessica's eyes. Once or twice she'd caught her mother looking at Jessica with a puzzled, almost troubled look. Elizabeth had held her breath, sure that the shinola was about to hit the fan. But it hadn't.

Finally she couldn't wait any longer. She heard Steven and Billie tiptoeing down the hall, and then her parents' door open. Tapping on Jessica's shoulder, she sang, "Get up, get up, you lazy pup," just the way Steven used to when they were little.

"Blow it out your ear, Steven," Jessica mumbled, flopping onto her other side.

Elizabeth laughed and shook Jessica's shoulder. "Jessica, come on, get up. It's Christmas."

Jessica's eyes popped open, and she looked at Elizabeth. "Why didn't you say so?" she cried, sliding out of bed. Her slippers were nowhere to be found, so she put on sweat socks. Two seconds later she had thrown on her robe and was struggling to shove her arms through the sleeves while trying to open Elizabeth's door. Then they raced downstairs together to the living room, where the tree was, and the gifts.

"Merry Christmas! Merry Christmas," everyone said, and they all exchanged hugs and kisses. Tom smiled when he saw Elizabeth, and she hugged him.

The day was cold and clear. As soon as Mrs. Wakefield had put on a pot of coffee, Jessica sat by the tree and began handing out presents.

"Mom, this is for you," she said, reading the label. She shook the package next to her ear. "Sounds like jewelry—a possible watch. Here." She handed the present to her mother and picked up another one. "Dad, here. Looks like Steven got you another tie. Hope it's better than last year's. Oh, here's one for me!" She put it aside. Soon all the gifts were distributed, and they each began un-

164

wrapping them. For an hour they exclaimed over their gifts, gasped in surprise, and thanked the givers warmly. Mr. Wakefield loved the book that Elizabeth had got him, and Tom exclaimed over his beautiful leather gloves. The girls each got gifts of clothes, books, and money. Steven and Billie got a large present to share: a bread maker. The final gift was for Elizabeth from Tom. It was a small box wrapped in gold paper and tied with silver ribbon. Holding her breath, she tore off the paper. Inside was a small jeweler's box, and she opened it slowly. Nestled against blue satin was a heart-shaped pendant on a gold chain. Inscribed on the heart was "I love you. Tom."

"Oh, Tom—it's beautiful!" Leaning over, she hugged him and gave him a kiss.

"I'm glad you like it," he said, pleased.

"I do. I love it."

Christmas dinner was traditionally served at two o'clock on Christmas Day, and at that time Mr. Wakefield triumphantly brought out the huge, beautifully cooked turkey.

Elizabeth and Jessica smiled at each other across the table.

Jessica felt a momentary sense of peacefulness, though she had no idea how long it would last. But right then, sitting at the table set with her mother's best china and crystal, the long green and red candles burning brightly, the silver gleaming, she felt as if the Christmas spirit had come to her at last.

Everyone watched as Mr. Wakefield carved the turkey. When each person had been served, and the other dishes passed around, Mr. Wakefield tapped on his wineglass. "I'd like to propose a toast," he said.

They all raised their glasses.

"To a year of new beginnings," Mr. Wakefield said in his deep baritone. "To my lovely daughters, who made their first semester of college such a success—I'm proud of you."

Jessica felt the blood drain from her face and knew that Elizabeth was looking at her in alarm.

"And to my son, who has honored me by following my footsteps into prelaw. I know you'll do well, Steven," Mr. Wakefield went on. "You're the most law-abiding and truthful person I know."

Across the table Steven choked on his wine.

Jessica fearfully raised her eyes in his direction. He was staring at his plate, looking unhappy and confused.

Oh no. He's going to tell.

"And a warm welcome to our two guests," Mr. Wakefield continued. "Billie, whom we have known for a while now and come to love. And to Tom, whose devotion to Elizabeth and courage in the newsroom will be legend for a long time to come."

"Hear, hear!"

Mrs. Wakefield turned to Jessica. "Oh, and Jessica?"

Jessica started. "What?"

"I have a little surprise for you after dinner."

166

Jessica wasn't sure whether to frown or to smile, so her face did something in·between.

"Bon appétit, everybody!" Mr. Wakefield declared. "And a very merry Christmas to all of us!"

As Tom swallowed his last piece of turkey, he breathed a sigh of relief. An entire meal gone by without a major disaster. Oh, he had splashed his share of cranberry sauce on the tablecloth. And there had been a momentary scare when the gravy boat was passed to him and he didn't realize it wasn't attached to the matching plate. But he'd managed to set it down without spilling the *entire* contents.

Just then the doorbell rang.

"I'll get it," Jessica said, heading for the front door. She opened the door to a blue-uniformed delivery man, who handed her a package. After reading the label, she returned to the dining room and handed the package to Elizabeth.

"It's for you," she said, obviously disappointed.

"Is that your surprise?" Elizabeth joked. "You get to accept a package for me?"

Jessica sighed. "I hope there's more to it than that."

Pushing the ribbons off, Elizabeth started to unwrap the package. She smiled at Tom, wondering if he had arranged another gift. But he looked concerned and almost worried, and she realized with a jolt that he hadn't sent it. Her fingers paused in the middle of tearing the wrapping as she remembered the scary phone call of two nights ago.

"Here, you do it like this," Jessica said, slicing a fingernail through the paper.

Brushing her aside, Elizabeth peeled apart the wrapping paper to uncover a small box. She flashed Tom a confused look, then lifted the lid.

Inside lay a beautiful hand-painted antique Christmas-tree angel. Not until she tried to lift it out did Elizabeth realize it had been shattered into three or four pieces.

"Oh, what a shame. It's broken," Mrs. Wakefield said over Elizabeth's shoulder.

"Who could have sent it?" Elizabeth asked, her eyes filled with wonder at the delicate and beautiful ornament. Then she saw something white peeking out from underneath. It was a note, folded into a small square. Turning away from the others, she unfolded it.

As she read the note, the blood drained from her face. Her hands began to shake.

If I can't have you, no one will.

"Elizabeth, what is it?" Mr. Wakefield asked. "You look like you've seen a ghost."

"Oh, nothing," Elizabeth said, smiling stiffly and crumpling the note in her hand.

"Don't worry, Elizabeth," her father said soothingly. "Tomorrow I'll try to glue the angel back together."

"Thanks, Dad," Elizabeth murmured.

Who is doing this to me? she wondered. She remembered something Todd had said to her a while ago, when she'd first started to receive these threatening messages.

"Maybe it's just some poor sucker who's hopelessly in love with you," he'd said. But it was the look in his eyes that she remembered now. It had been a confused look, sorrowful. . . .

Sorrowful—or guilty?

What on earth could my surprise be? Jessica wondered. She kept waiting for her mother to bring out a new gift, but everyone was just sitting around the living room, looking at all their presents. Frowning, she took another sip of her coffee.

The doorbell rang again, and everyone looked up in surprise.

Except Mrs. Wakefield. Her eyes twinkling, she said, "Jessica, could you get that for me, please?"

Suddenly Jessica knew what her surprise was. It was James! He must have called yesterday while she was out shopping and arranged the whole thing with her mother. A smile lit her face as she flew toward the door.

In the foyer she grabbed for the doorknob and yanked the door open. The outside light was off, and the streetlight behind the figure had cast a shadow on his face. Her smile broadened as she reached out to pull James inside.

The figure stepped forward. Not strongly or confidently, but slowly and with a slight limp.

Suddenly Jessica stumbled backward, her eyes

169

as big as saucers. She clapped a hand over her mouth to keep from shrieking out loud. Standing as still as statues, she and Mike stared at each other in dead silence for a moment that seemed to Jessica to last an eternity.

Standing in the Wakefields' doorway, Mike swallowed hard. From Jessica's expression it was pretty clear that what she felt was not surprise and elation, but fear and shock. His fist clenched in his pocket around the small velvet box there.

"Oops, wrong house," he said dryly. "I guess I'll be going." He turned to leave.

"Who is it, dear?" Alice Wakefield called from the foyer. She appeared in the doorway. "Is that Mike?"

Mike stopped and turned back toward the house.

"It looks like a bad time, Mrs. Wakefield," he said, gazing longingly at Jessica. "You all must be busy. . . ."

"Don't be silly," Mrs. Wakefield said quickly. "Come on in. You're just in time for coffee."

Mike looked to Jessica for some sign, some word that would tell him what to do. But all she could do was gape at him, her eyes wide, her face pale. He'd forgotten that she hadn't seen him walk in weeks, not since the shooting. Not since the night she had left him. As far as she was concerned, he'd been paralyzed for life.

Mike took a hesitant step toward Mrs. Wakefield's outstretched hand. After the forty-five-minute drive, his legs felt weak. His knees almost buckled, and he stumbled toward the house.

"Oh, my goodness!" Mrs. Wakefield. "Why, you're limping! Have you had an accident?"

"Yes," Mike said, then quickly added, "a motorcycle accident. But I'm recovering."

"Watch your step," Mrs. Wakefield said soothingly, helping Mike across the threshold and into the hall.

As he walked in, he brushed by Jessica. He smelled her hair, and all that had once been familiar to him came flooding back. Their short marriage passed before his eyes instantaneously, and it was all he could do to keep himself from jerking in pain.

Slowly he followed Mrs. Wakefield and Jessica into the living room. A Christmas tree reached to the ceiling in one corner. Opened packages filled with gifts made a huge pile under the tree. *Just like a Rockwell painting.*

Mike had prepared himself for a traumatic entrance, but as Jessica and her mother parted to let everyone else see who it was at the door, he realized that nothing could have equipped him to deal with the reality.

A man who must be Jessica's father rose and came toward him with an outstretched hand. Elizabeth was just looking at him in shock, and Billie raised her eyebrows at him. Some guy Mike didn't know leaned over to ask Elizabeth what was going on.

And Steven said, "Mike!"

"Oh, you know Jessica's friend, too, Steven?"

Mrs. Wakefield asked. "That's nice. Did you meet at SVU?"

There was a long, painful, suspended silence. Elizabeth and Tom squirmed in their seats. Jessica and Steven shifted their weight from one foot to the other.

Then Mike switched on a warm, pleasant smile, as if he were flipping on a light.

"No, not at SVU," Mike said confidently. "Steven and I met at the mechanic's shop when we were both having work done on our cars. We got to talking . . ."

"Oh, and he introduced you to Jessica; I get it!" Mrs. Wakefield said with a smile.

"R-right!" Steven blurted, with a relieved but still pained look in his eyes.

"Please, make yourself comfortable, Mike," Mr. Wakefield said, stepping out of the way and offering Mike a chair. "I'll get you a cup of coffee."

"Thanks," Mike said politely, sitting down. *So these were my in-laws,* he thought as Mr. Wakefield left for the kitchen and Mrs. Wakefield took her place between Billie and Elizabeth. *They seem like pretty decent folks. I bet if our marriage hadn't been such a big secret, if this family had been involved, we could have made it. They would have pulled us through.*

Mike looked from face to face, smiling pleasantly. To her credit, even Elizabeth met his gaze and nodded. In her eyes he saw not hatred, but worry. She was worried he had come to hurt

Jessica again. A small frown creased his brow. He couldn't blame her. But maybe one day in the future, after he had mended all the damage he had caused, after he had devoted his life to making Jessica happy, Elizabeth would forgive him.

"So, Mike," Mr. Wakefield began, handing Mike his coffee. "Did I hear you say you'd been in a motorcycle accident? I hope that convinced you to give up motorcycles for good."

"Yes, sir, it did. I'm done with that wild stuff," Mike announced clearly, hoping Jessica would understand that he was talking about having changed in more ways than one. As Jessica raised her head in his direction, he saw he'd got her attention.

"Everyone has to grow up sometime," Mike went on. "The . . . accident made me realize it was my time. In some ways it was one of the best things that ever happened to me." Across the room he met Steven's concerned gaze.

"Good for you," Mr. Wakefield said. "Everyone deserves a new start once in his life. Here's to yours." He lifted his cup of coffee, and so did everyone else, with varying degrees of enthusiasm.

Mike met Jessica's eyes over the rim of his cup as he drank.

Jessica looked back at him as if she didn't believe what she was seeing.

Sitting back in his chair, he looked around the room, feeling both strangely comfortable and ill at ease at the same time. *They never knew I was once their family, their son-in-law. Maybe . . .* He gazed deeply at Jessica, who was more beautiful than ever. *Maybe it's not too late for me to be again.*

Elizabeth anxiously watched Jessica from across the room. Her twin was sitting stiffly, a nervous smile glued to her face. Suddenly Elizabeth felt a deep weariness. She was glad to be home for Christmas, but the visit had also been very trying emotionally. It was exhausting having to watch everything she said in order to keep Jessica's marriage secret. In addition, she'd had to buoy Tom's feelings constantly, since he was so insecure about what her parents thought of him. And to top it all off, there had been that strained, ridiculous scene in the mall yesterday with Todd and Alexandra, who might or might not be dating.

Her head ached, and Elizabeth pressed her fingers to her temples. Maybe she shouldn't have had that second cup of coffee. It felt as if her blood were pounding through her brain. She thought if she had to sit there for one more minute watching Mike McAllery try to charm her parents—and apparently succeeding—she was going to scream.

What she desperately needed was some time alone. Time when she didn't have to talk or smile or be polite or take care of anyone's feelings but her own. She leaned over to Tom, sitting next to her. "Come to the kitchen for a minute," she whispered.

They excused themselves as casually as possible. Once in the kitchen, Tom asked, "What's wrong?"

"I don't know," Elizabeth said, feeling confused and impatient. "That whole scene in there is giving me the willies."

"Yeah. But Jessica seems pretty determined to keep him out of her life. I bet she'll be OK." Soothingly Tom stroked Elizabeth's hair.

For no good reason she felt smothered, suffocated. She shook her head clear and realized that Tom was still standing with her, waiting for her to respond. "Tom," she said, searching his eyes, "I really need a few minutes alone. Could you please tell my folks that I went for a quick walk?"

He looked down at her, confused. "Let me come with you."

Shaking her head, Elizabeth said, "I'm sorry, Tom. I know it's rude of me to leave you here, but please understand. I just really need a few moments to clear my head. OK?"

After a minute of hesitation Tom said, "Of course. I understand. It has been kind of tense around here. For you, especially."

Gratitude filled her heart. "Thanks, Tom. You're the best." She leaned up and kissed him quickly, then grabbed her coat off a kitchen chair. "I won't be long."

"Just be careful," Tom warned her. "Don't go too far by yourself."

"Promise."

Once outside, she breathed in deeply. The relief was almost overwhelming—the coolness of the early evening, the moonlight washing over her, the silence: It was like diving into a cool pool on a burning-hot summer's day.

The neighborhood was aglow in Christmas lights. Most of the houses on the block had Christmas trees displayed in their front windows. Elizabeth saw some of her neighbors through the glass. From the outside everyone looked so happy. . . . *I wonder if everyone really is.*

She passed the Piedmonts', and their gaudy decorations made her smile. For as long as she could remember, the Piedmonts had decorated their house to within an inch of its life at Christmas. When she and Jessica had been little, they had begged their parents to do the same.

A memory came to Elizabeth of her and Todd, one year ago today. They had walked down her street, hand in hand. They had stopped in front of the Piedmonts' and admired the outrageous decorations, laughing together.

Was it really a whole year ago? she wondered, wiping her eyes. *Sometimes it seems like yesterday.* Her hands in her pockets and her collar up against the Christmas chill, Elizabeth walked by instinct, following a route that was so familiar, she could have walked it in her sleep.

In a few minutes she found herself in a place that was burned in her memory. The little neighborhood park. She and Jessica had played there when they were little. Later she and Todd had spent many hours there alone. Without meaning to, she headed for the large tree with the bench beneath it. They had come here so often last summer. And for the last several years they had exchanged their Christmas gifts beneath their tree.

Sorry, Todd, she thought with a mixture of bitterness and sadness. *I didn't get you anything this year.*

A noise broke into Elizabeth's melancholy reverie, a rustle in the leaves. She froze. A soft breeze picked up and blew her hair in front her eyes.

Someone coughed softly.

"Who's there?" she called into the darkness, remembering all too late the frightening phone call, the broken Christmas angel. It had been stupid to come out alone, to wander in a dark park by herself. What had she been thinking?

Her throat closed when she saw a dark figure separate from the stand of trees and move toward her.

Chapter Fifteen

Finally alone with Mike, Jessica sat stiffly in an easy chair in the family room. Mike was across the room on the couch, looking uncomfortable, but there was a glint of determination in his golden eyes.

Memories flooded Jessica's mind. *How did we ever get to this point?* Just a month ago she'd thought she'd known Mike—knew him intimately, knew everything about him. Now, sitting silently, she felt as if she had no idea who he was.

She remembered his motorcycle, the feel of the wind whipping against her face as they shot through the night. She remembered his powerful arms lifting her into the air, cradling her, carrying her over the threshold of his apartment into the safety of his bed. She remembered what had happened next.

Blinking, Jessica took a deep breath. Before her was a different Mike. He was a little thin, but almost back to his normal weight. There was something different in his eyes. They seemed more searching, less confident.

Right now Jessica was torn between wanting to kill him for showing up, and being grateful because he hadn't given her secret away in front of her parents.

"I can't believe we survived that," Jessica murmured, shaking her head.

"Me neither," Mike said, attempting a weak smile.

"I knew you were a good liar," Jessica said ruefully, "but I didn't know you were that good."

A flash of pain showed in his eyes for a moment. "I hate the idea of your thinking of me that way," he said hoarsely. "Jess, I came to tell you that the lying days are over."

"Funny, it doesn't seem that way to me," Jessica interrupted him.

He shrugged in frustration. "I did it so I could see you. From now on I only want truth between us."

"What *is* the truth, Mike?"

Mike pierced her with those hazel eyes. Jessica looked away quickly, afraid of being bewitched, just like the first day she had seen him. They'd met, and she'd fallen helplessly into his arms.

"Your parents are great, Jess," Mike said. "They'd be great in-laws."

Jessica looked down at the floor. Vaguely she realized that all traces of Tom's chocolate-cake fiasco had been removed. She almost smiled. Then she took a deep breath. Mike was still there. What did he want? It was over between them.

"Mike—I'm glad you can walk again," Jessica began hesitantly. "I hated the idea of your being . . . hurt for the rest of your life. But we had an agreement. You let me go." She kept her voice low in case anyone could overhear them.

Mike winced slightly. "Jessica, I came to apologize to you. I know I was a bastard and made your life hell. But I've changed, I swear it. Jess—I never stopped loving you. Even when we had the marriage annulled," he said bitterly, "I still loved you. But I couldn't tie you to someone who was paralyzed. That's changed now. I'm going to be fully recovered in another month or two. And I've changed inside, too. I just want the chance to prove it to you."

Flushing, Jessica looked at him. This was the most painful thing she'd ever had to go through in her life. She had no idea what to say. Intellectually she thought she wanted him to walk out of the house and never speak to her again. But emotionally, every time she looked into his eyes, she saw a little part of herself. A memory of herself in love.

Before she could speak, Mike reached into his pocket and pulled out a small velvet box. He got up from his chair and moved in front of her, where he knelt on the floor at her feet.

Feeling as if she were in a dream, Jessica looked at him in disbelief. When she made no move to take the box, he opened it for her and held it out.

Her jaw fell open. Inside, a huge diamond solitaire flamed and sparkled.

It must have cost a fortune. "What is this?" she whispered, staring at the ring.

Mike held up his hand. "Jessica, I regret not doing things the right way the first time around. You deserve a real engagement ring, and a huge wedding with flowers and music and all of your friends and your family there to celebrate with you."

"Oh, Mike . . ."

"This time I promise to give you everything you want. Everything you deserve."

She couldn't believe what she was hearing. A month ago this would have made her the happiest woman on the face of the earth. Now it only threw her into an emotional tailspin that she wasn't sure she'd ever recover from.

"Mike, our marriage was annulled. I can't believe that you'd change so much in such a short time. We agreed not to see each other again."

Wordlessly Mike took her left hand and gently slid the ring on the third finger.

"Your parents didn't know about the first time," he said softly. "But I want everyone to know about this one. Will you give me a second chance? Jessica, I'm begging you to let me make you happy. What do you say? Will you marry me?"

Alexandra Rollins smiled with pleasure as she saw her mother wearing the cranberry wool sweater Alexandra had given her for Christmas.

She was lying on the living-room couch, listening to Christmas carols and reflecting on what a nice day it had been. Earlier she had talked to Todd. He was still in a bad way, but she could tell his parents were trying to be supportive and nonjudgmental. Though of course they must be horrified and disappointed with how Todd's life had changed recently, Alexandra thought.

But there was something missing, something that wasn't quite right about today. Although she tried to pretend that she didn't know what it was, deep inside she really did. It was Elizabeth. She was missing. For practically as long as she could remember, no matter what, they had exchanged gifts on Christmas. This year she hadn't even bought Elizabeth anything. It felt weird.

When college had first started, Alexandra had seized life in both hands for the first time. She'd changed her name, her image, her looks, everything about her life. At the same time, Elizabeth had been overwhelmed by college, and had reacted by desperately trying to keep everything around her the same. They hadn't fit together, they had nothing in common. They'd drifted apart, and then when Mark had been expelled, Alexandra had blamed Elizabeth publicly. That had been the end of years of friendship.

Or had it? Alexandra rolled into a sitting position, regretting that second piece of pecan pie. Now she and Elizabeth didn't seem as different as they had at the beginning of the year. Now she missed Elizabeth more than she ever thought she would. Now she needed a best friend in the worst way. And no matter what anyone could say about Elizabeth, she'd always been the best friend Alexandra had ever had.

Alexandra licked her lips. What about Todd? What would Elizabeth think about it if Alexandra and Todd did actually start dating? Elizabeth had always had everything: beauty, intelligence, warmth—and Todd. Now it seemed that Alexandra had a shot at some of those things too. She wasn't sure whether she and Todd would develop their relationship or not, but she knew she wanted the chance. The reunion was tomorrow, and Alexandra desperately wanted to shake everyone up—all those people who remembered her as dull, predictable Enid Rollins. To show up with Todd . . . that would really be something. People would have to take her seriously.

Quietly, Alexandra lay back down on the couch and picked up the book her father had given her. She missed Elizabeth, but she had to put herself first.

"Who's there?" Elizabeth called into the dark, trying to sound brave and confident. Blurred images of being abducted by the secret society raced through her mind, and she tried to banish them.

"Elizabeth? Is that you?"

Todd. At the sound of the familiar voice, Elizabeth almost wept with relief. For some reason she wasn't surprised that Todd was there. It was almost as if she'd known he would be.

She remembered the last time they were at the park together. It was the night before they were to leave for college, the last night of their old life. They'd gone on a last date to all their favorite places, beginning with a romantic dinner at the Box Tree Café and ending with a milk shake at the Dairi Burger. Then they had come to their private place in this little park. Lying on the grass in each other's arms, they'd shared their dreams for the future and for each other.

That seemed so long ago now. Both their lives had changed so much. Then Elizabeth thought of the phone call, the broken angel. Was Tom right? Was Todd so bitter and jealous that he would hurt her? She didn't think so. But one thing she'd learned during her first semester of college was that she really didn't know anyone as well as she'd thought. Including Jessica, her very own twin.

"Funny running into you here," she said neutrally. In the dim light she could barely make out his features, but he seemed older somehow. His easy, carefree manner was gone, perhaps forever, to be replaced by disappointment and bitterness. Yet his face, the way he stood, everything about him was hauntingly familiar.

"I needed to get out of the house," Todd replied, also neutrally. He sat down on the cool cement bench, not asking her to join him.

Below them the lights of Sweet Valley winked like the stars of an upside-down sky.

"Me too," Elizabeth replied soberly. "It's a beautiful night, at least."

"How are things at the Wakefield *casa*?" Todd asked. "Have a good Christmas?"

"Oh, well . . ." Elizabeth stopped, confused. Actually, she couldn't honestly say that it had been a good Christmas. Sure, she'd gotten lots of great presents, but things at home were so weird and strained. . . .

There had been a time when Elizabeth would have told Todd everything, every detail. He would have listened thoughtfully and comforted her. She felt a sudden urge to tell him everything now, everything about the mess with Jessica and Mike and Steven. But she didn't. Instead she sat down next to him on the bench, gingerly, keeping her distance. He glanced at her but didn't say anything.

"Todd," Elizabeth said suddenly, "did you call my house yesterday?"

Todd looked at her blankly. "Call your house? No."

"Or have anything delivered tonight?"

"No," he said, a twinge of bitterness in his voice. "Why?"

Maybe it was his tone of voice, maybe it was just wishful thinking—but whatever it was, Elizabeth was sure Todd was telling the truth. She felt an enormous weight lift off her shoulders. She felt so relieved, she almost laughed.

"Todd, are you coming back to school?" she asked almost timidly.

"No."

"But you'll be reinstated on the team next year," Elizabeth said. She knew it wasn't any of her business, not anymore, but she couldn't stop herself. "The dean said you can practice with them now."

"Yeah, yeah." Todd sounded tired, and her heart went out to him.

She waited, unsure of what to say.

"I don't see the point of going back," he said finally.

Elizabeth couldn't believe this was Todd talking. She really didn't know him, after all. "What about your goals?" she asked, feeling as if she were treading on thin ice. "Your college degree? You used to seem so determined. You know, you could train hard all next semester, get in top shape, and come back next year and be the star of the team."

Todd laughed a little and started twirling a stick in his hands.

Suddenly Elizabeth felt involved in his life, as though she had a stake in what he did with his future—just the way she had when they were going out.

"All your friends are in school. You don't want to be left behind," she said in a small voice.

He looked at her then. "What do you care?" he asked, but without rancor. Then, as though realizing the unfairness of the question, he threw the stick into the darkness. "Ah, it doesn't matter anyway. I just blew off all my exams. There's no way I could salvage last semester."

"So get incompletes," Elizabeth said practically. "Next semester, since you won't be on the team, you'll have extra time to study. By next spring you'll be doing OK in your regular courses, and you'll have finished all your incompletes too." She felt excited, happy. She realized she desperately wanted Todd to do well. But she didn't know why. "You've got to give yourself another chance."

Looking at him, she saw the confusion and longing in his brown eyes. The moonlight highlighted his dark hair.

"Will you, Todd?" Elizabeth asked softly. "Will you give yourself another chance?"

Todd didn't answer, just stared at her in the darkness as though he were seeing a vision.

"Why did you come here, Elizabeth?" he asked quietly.

She looked up. "I don't know," she lied. It would take no effort just to lean forward one, two inches and kiss him, as she had so many times before.

What am I doing? Todd is out of my life, and I like it that way. It's Tom I love, it's Tom, it's Tom, she repeated to herself.

Standing quickly, she brushed a bit of dried leaf off her jacket. "I wish you'd think about what I've said."

"Maybe I will," he answered quietly. "Heading back now?"

"Yeah," she said breathlessly. "I better get back."

"OK. Merry Christmas."

The sadness in his voice almost ripped her heart in two, but she forced herself to smile and nod. "Yes. Merry Christmas, Todd. I'm glad I— well, I'm glad I saw you. Take care."

Then she walked back home hurriedly, not daring to look back.

Chapter Sixteen

I don't believe this is happening, Jessica thought frantically. She stared down at the huge diamond on her ring finger in disbelief.

"Mike, I thought everything was over between us," she said, feeling as though her mind were spinning.

"Jessica, I'll do anything you want," Mike said. He sat on a chair next to her and took both her hands in his. "I've been thinking about our future. Of course, I want you to finish college, and I'm going to help you. And I promise that there will be no more lying, no more drinking, no more running around. You'll be proud of me—you'll see. I'll do anything you want to make you happy."

"Mike—" Jessica's voice stuck in her throat, and she gave a little cough. Then, feeling an almost unbearable ache of sadness in her chest, she slowly took the ring off her finger. "It's a beautiful ring, Mike. I really think you *have* changed, and I'm happy about it. But we split up for a big reason, and that reason hasn't changed."

She held the ring out to him, and when he didn't take it, she pried open his fingers, put the ring in his palm, and closed his hand around it. "Mike, it wasn't just the fighting and arguing and yelling that broke us up. We're just—different people. A lot of it was my fault."

Mike started to protest, but she silenced him with a look. "Mike, I'm only eighteen years old. I have my whole life ahead of me. Being an independent college woman is part of that life. I'm just not ready to be a wife—to anyone. Eighteen is just too young for me to settle down with someone forever. And the next time I get married," she said, barely whispering, "if I *do* get married again, I want it to be forever." Tears glistened in her eyes, and she swallowed hard. Looking into Mike's eyes, she saw the pain there that mirrored her own.

"Why don't you just think about it for a while," he suggested in a low voice. "Keep the ring as long as you want. Maybe—"

"Mike, I'm sorry. I'm *sorry*—more sorry than you'll ever know. But it's over between us."

When Jessica heard the front door slam, and then Elizabeth's voice, she knew that she couldn't put off her decision any longer. Mike wasn't the only one who had changed, she thought, feeling a sense of dread about what she was going to do. She had changed, too. Being married had changed her forever. Now she had to prove it to herself, to Elizabeth, to Steven, to her parents. It was going to be horrible, she admitted to herself. It might affect the way her family felt about her forever. But sometimes that happened in families, and it might happen to her tonight.

She had thought long and hard about her decision. In some ways she supposed that she'd known she would have to do this for a long time. The last few days had shown her that until she made a clean breast of it, her life would be a lie. Every smile her parents gave her, every time they felt happy about her, would just be false, unless they knew.

Jessica took a deep breath and stood, feeling shaky. Opening Elizabeth's door, she headed downstairs. She'd never wanted to do anything less in her life. If there was a way out of it, she'd take it—as long as it didn't involve lying to her parents. She'd done a lot of thinking, up in Elizabeth's room by herself, since Mike had left. All her life she'd been the irresponsible one, the one who got into scrapes. It was just how she was—she couldn't help it. But this was the biggest thing in her life, and she couldn't just pretend it away. And she knew now that there was no way she could let her parents hear about it from someone else.

In the family room Elizabeth and Mrs. Wakefield were looking through a glossy gardening book

191

that Mr. Wakefield had given his wife. The other four were playing cards, and Billie was accusing Steven of cheating.

Jessica swallowed hard. It took every ounce of self-control not to run out of the room and back upstairs. She would have given anything in that moment not to have to do what she was about to do.

Elizabeth looked up, smiled, then seemed to notice Jessica's face. In an instant Jessica saw horror on her twin's face.

Jessica swallowed hard again. "Mom, Dad, I have something to tell you." She saw Steven start in surprise, and Billie frown concernedly. "You guys already know this, so you can stay," she said with a wave of her hand.

"Jessica—are you sure?" Steven said quietly.

Meeting his eyes bravely, she nodded, though her knees were quaking. "Yes." Turning to her parents, she said, "Mike came by today to ask me to marry him." Elizabeth made a choking sound, but Jessica kept her gaze on her parents.

"Marry—! Oh . . . I see," Mrs. Wakefield said carefully. "But you feel that you're too young for marriage, don't you, sweetie?"

Sitting down on the couch next to Elizabeth, Jessica gripped her hands in her lap until they were white. "Yes, I do," she said clearly. Then her head bowed, and her long hair obscured her face. "But I didn't a month ago. You see—Mike was really asking me to *re*marry him. A month ago we were wed by a justice of the peace."

"What?" Mr. Wakefield said loudly.

Jessica forced herself to stay calm. Her mother had one hand to her throat but was silent. "The marriage was annulled last week."

"Jessica," Mrs. Wakefield said faintly, "are you saying you got married? While we were out of town?" She looked around the room as if for confirmation. "My daughter got married without me? I—I don't know what to say."

"There's more," Jessica plowed on. "Of course, the marriage was rocky from the beginning. I'm much too young, and Mike . . . was different from how he was tonight. We fought a lot. And . . . we lived downstairs from Steven and Billie." Looking up, she met Steven's eyes. He looked sober, but he nodded. "Anyway, one night we were fighting a lot, and I ran to Steven's . . ." Jessica could feel her throat closing. "Mike followed me," she said hoarsely. "He had a gun." Mrs. Wakefield gasped, and her husband came to stand beside her, holding her hand. "Steven got into a fight with Mike, and the gun went off. Mike wasn't in a motorcycle accident, Mom. The bullet hit his spine, and he was paralyzed."

"Oh, my God," Mrs. Wakefield whispered.

Steven cleared his throat. "I . . . got arrested, because Mike and I had been wrestling over the gun. The judge sentenced me to help Mike with his rehabilitation. So I did. Then, a few days ago, Mike saved my life. It's a long story, but I almost died of gas poisoning. That night Mike realized

193

that he was regaining feeling in his legs, and now he's recovered a great deal, as you saw tonight. In another month or two he'll be fine."

Her brother took a deep breath, and Jessica continued, conscious of her mother's white face, and her father's intense frown. "So Mike feels that he's changed a lot for the better. He came here to apologize to me, and to ask me to give him another chance."

"And you said no?" Mrs. Wakefield said in a very soft, very strained voice.

"I said no. I care about Mike, but there's no way I'll get married again for a long, long time. I just want to focus on school. And now I have to apologize to you, Mom and Dad, for being so amazingly stupid, and for being such a disappointment to you . . . and a failure as a daughter. I'll understand if you hate me, or if you want to kick me out," she finished in a whisper. Her eyes filled with tears and she dashed them away. She meant to be brave and mature, and here she was about to break down completely.

"I—I just can't quite take all this in," Mrs. Wakefield said faintly. "I just can't believe it somehow." She looked from Jessica to Steven. "Both of you, keeping this from us, not trusting us, lying to us. And tonight I let Mike in and treated him as a guest. . . ." Looking white with shock, Mrs. Wakefield's voice wavered and trailed off, and tears started running down her cheeks. She didn't seem to notice.

"Why did I even bother as a father?" Mr. Wakefield said, anger creeping into his voice. "When I think of all we tried to do for you, all the values I'd hoped we'd instilled. Well, let me tell you, my dreams of that are shot."

Burying her face in her hands, Jessica began sobbing. Elizabeth put her arms around her and held her head. "Dad, believe me, she's paid enough," Elizabeth said.

"You keep out of it. Unless you have some mind-shattering secret you want to share with us too," her father snapped.

"No!" Elizabeth said. "But Jessica knows she made a huge mistake. She's paid for it. Now she knows it was wrong. Steven and I agreed to keep it quiet, but she decided to tell you. Doesn't that mean anything to you?"

"Yes. It means all three of my children have betrayed my trust," Mr. Wakefield said coldly. "Disappointed me, and embarrassed me. Now if you'll excuse us, I think your mother needs to lie down."

Mrs. Wakefield was sobbing as hard as Jessica was, and her husband put his arm around her and helped her stand. With a final backward glare they left the room and went upstairs.

"Shh," Elizabeth soothed Jessica. "You did the right thing, Jess. It's going to be OK. We're just growing up, is all."

Across the room she met Tom's eyes. He was gazing at her compassionately.

195

"I just want to die," Jessica sobbed. "I wish I'd never come home."

Steven came over and also wrapped his arms around her, and Billie came to hover worriedly. "You did the right thing, Jessica," he confirmed. "I know Mom and Dad are really upset right now, but life will go on. They'll get over it. You're still their daughter, and they love you."

"Steven's right," Elizabeth said. "It'll all be better tomorrow. You'll see." But in her heart, she had no idea if that was true.

Lila was awakened by Susan, the maid, tiptoeing into her room with her breakfast tray.

"Morning, Susan," Lila mumbled sleepily. Susan set down the tray and opened Lila's curtains. It was a cloudy winter day, rare in Sweet Valley. Sitting up, Lila poured herself coffee from the miniature china pot, then uncovered her plate to find some hot apricot croissants. Susan left silently as Lila began her breakfast.

She had slept well the night before, she realized gratefully. No nightmares, no dreams of Tisiano or of flying. Cheerfully Lila applied herself to a croissant. Then she remembered that tonight was her high-school reunion. *Ugh.* No doubt everyone would stare at her, whispering comments about her hasty marriage and just as hasty widowhood. *Widow.* It was such an ugly word, full of sorrow, full of pain.

A defiant look in her eye, Lila tossed back her

long dark hair. She knew what people would be expecting tonight. But she wasn't going to give it to them. Instead of the pathetic Widow Fowler, dressed in black, pale, weeping, she would give them a taste of the Fowler strength. Tonight when she breezed into the reunion, she would look like the million bucks she was worth, or more. There was no way she'd leave herself open to prying questions and sympathetic comments. Jessica would have to help her. Together they would be carefree, beautiful, the life of the party. Just like old times.

Jessica opened one eye, then the other. Immediately she turned and faced Elizabeth. Her twin had just woken up also.

"Tell me last night was just a bad dream," Jessica asked.

"I wish I could," Elizabeth whispered. "But it wasn't. You know, Jessica, last night you did the bravest thing I've ever seen you do. I'm proud of you. But today we both have to be brave: We have to go downstairs and face them."

"Poor Tom," Jessica sighed. "I bet he didn't know he was going to spend his Christmas holidays in the middle of a horrible Wakefield drama."

Elizabeth managed a weak smile. "He'll live."

Though she tried to look strong, for Elizabeth's sake, a black cloud settled around Jessica's heart. After the scene the night before, her parents hadn't come downstairs again. As horrible as it had been last night, she knew that today, as they all faced the aftermath of her revelation, could be even worse. But she knew she had to see her parents again, even if it was just to say good-bye before she left. Would they still pay for her college? Well, she could get a job—she was determined to finish her education. But the prospect seemed incredibly bleak.

"I split our family apart, Elizabeth," Jessica said sadly. "I've caused a rift so deep that nothing will ever fill it. They'll never forgive me. Our family will never be the same again—and it's all my fault." She felt tears come into her eyes again.

"Don't say that, Jessica," Elizabeth said, climbing out of bed. "Families have problems. They work them out. Together, we'll get through this, too. Whatever happens, you know that I'll always be on your side." Feeling pangs of gratitude, Jessica hugged her twin.

Creeping downstairs, they listened to the muffled sounds from the kitchen. Then they took deep breaths, squeezed each other's hands, and went in. Mr. and Mrs. Wakefield were sitting at the kitchen table, eating breakfast as though it were an ordinary day. Alice Wakefield looked pale and subdued, and perhaps a few years older. There were lines of tension around Ned Wakefield's mouth and on his forehead.

Steven was already there as well, but Billie and Tom had thoughtfully not put in an entrance yet. Jessica looked at Steven curiously. He was reading the sports section and working on a sweet roll. When they came in, he looked up and threw them a wink.

"Morning," Elizabeth said hesitantly.

Their parents looked up.

"Good morning," their mother said. Though her voice sounded strained, there seemed to be no evidence of anger. Jessica saw her father meeting her mother's eyes. Feeling as though her throat were closing up, she and Elizabeth sat down.

"Jessica, Elizabeth. I guess it would be best if I just got it all out into the open this morning." Meeting Jessica's eyes, he gave a rueful smile. "I don't think life can go on until we all make up."

"I think that's true," Jessica whispered, looking down at her place mat.

Her father reached out and took her hand. To Jessica it felt like the touch of life. "Look," he began, "we all said a lot of things last night. What you told us about your marriage really shocked me, and yes, disappointed me as well. And I was upset that your mother was upset." He paused, seeming not to know how to go on.

Mrs. Wakefield broke in. "Well, we were very upset," she repeated. "It was a real—surprise. I just didn't know how to react. Then, later, when we talked about it, we realized a few things." She reached across the table and took Jessica's other hand. "My main feeling is I wish you felt you could have told us, sweetheart. I wish you had sent a telegram or something. I wish you had called and said, 'Mom, come home. I need you.'" She paused and took a deep breath. "Don't you know by now you can tell us anything? You're our daughter; we love you. That means no matter what."

Jessica felt overwhelmed by emotion and started crying again. She felt Elizabeth shifting her seat next to her.

"Jessica," Mr. Wakefield said quietly, "last night was awful for all of us, but no one has been through more than you. A door has opened for you, and a door has closed. It was awful for me to realize you're not daddy's little girl anymore. You're an adult. You've known the responsibility of marriage, and though it didn't work out, you dealt with it responsibly. Actually, I'm proud of you, Jessica."

Mr. Wakefield leaned over and hugged his daughter. "Later we're going to want to hear more of the gruesome details, when you feel ready to tell us. But for right now all I want to say is I love you, and I always will."

"Oh, Daddy!" Jessica sobbed. And though she knew she wasn't daddy's little girl anymore, it still felt good to be in her father's arms. It felt like home.

"OK, guys," Steven said in a ludicrously sappy voice, "group hug!" He pushed back his chair and stood up with his arms out, a smarmy smile on his face. Laughing, Elizabeth stood and hugged him, and they were joined by their parents and Jessica.

"All together now," Steven chirped. "I love you," he sang, "you love me, we're a happy fam-i-ly. . . ."

"Steven, shut up!" Mrs. Wakefield cried, then hugged her family harder.

Chapter Seventeen

As the sun set in a rainbow of blues and pinks outside the window, Elizabeth and Jessica stood side by side in matching fluffy bath sheets at the bathroom sink. Makeup and hair accessories were spread before them like surgeon's instruments. It was time for the reunion.

Elizabeth had decided on a simple blue silk jumpsuit that matched her eyes and set off her long golden-blond hair. Jessica pulled a box from Lisette's out from under the bed and held up a devastatingly sexy black Lycra micromini.

"Are you going to paint that on or *put* it on?" Elizabeth asked. No matter how much alike they looked, their styles would always be opposite.

Jessica smirked.

"So what time is James picking you up?" Elizabeth asked, smoothing on foundation.

"Eight thirty," Jessica replied, opening her makeup bag.

"But the reunion starts at *seven* thirty," Elizabeth pointed out.

Jessica rolled her eyes. "Calm down, Liz," she mouthed around her lipstick tube. "It's *boring* to show up on time for a big party like this."

Elizabeth chuckled as her twin tossed her head and struck a dramatic cover-girl pose in front of the mirror. She began dabbing on some lip gloss with the tip of her pinkie, then stopped and stared at herself in the mirror.

"What's wrong, Elizabeth?" Jessica asked. "Can't decide between raspberry ice or peach frost?"

"Uh, not exactly." *How do I ask her?* Elizabeth wondered. The question had been plaguing her for weeks, ever since she and Tom had begun to get more and more serious. She decided to dive in. "Uh, Jessica? Can I ask you something?"

"Shoot." Jessica fastened on her dramatic silver earrings.

"Well, Tom and I . . . I mean, well, you know—you've had sex. What's it like?" she blurted.

Jessica smiled knowingly. "Tom Terrific making headway, is he?" Then her gaze softened. "Well, to be perfectly honest, Liz," she said, her voice filled with a maturity that was odd to hear, "it's a little strange at first. I mean, it's not all thunder and lightning, you know."

Elizabeth blushed with embarrassment.

"It isn't the same for everyone," Jessica continued. "All the movies and romance novels make you think the earth is going to move and it's going to be perfect every time. But that's a fantasy. The two most important things are that you really love the person and really trust him totally. But I guess that won't be a problem with you and Tom."

Elizabeth nodded.

"And, of course, use birth control." Jessica frowned into the mirror. "Do you like these earrings?"

"Jessica!"

Jessica leaned over and hugged her sister. "Look—you'll find out for yourself. If you love Tom and trust him, and he loves and trusts you, everything will be fine. And if it isn't, come back to me and we'll talk again. OK?"

"OK," Elizabeth agreed, her eyes shining. She looked into the mirror and marveled at how much alike they really were. Their hair was sun-streaked in the same places, their dimples were in the same corner of their left cheeks. She realized how much they took each other for granted. But this Christmas had shown her how thankful they were to have each other. The last measure of the holiday's tension melted out of her body, and a feeling of utter well-being and happiness took its place. It was a beautiful night, and Sweet Valley was the perfect place to come home to. Now she and Jessica were going to dance the night away at their high-school reunion.

At this moment Elizabeth felt she couldn't be more content.

*   *   *

When the doorbell rang, Alexandra was ready and waiting. "I'll get it!" she called, then ran to the front door. Flinging it open, she looked deeply into Todd's eyes.

"Hey," he said, then paused, seeming to realize suddenly who she was. Slowly his eyes looked her up and down.

Alexandra held her breath. In the end she had decided on a crinkly black baby-doll dress over a slinky black slip. The square neckline was cut low, and the sleeves were long and full and ruffled. The dress's skirt skimmed her calves, but the slip ended well above her knees, and every time she moved, the barest glimpse of her legs showed through the fabric. Makeup enhanced her green eyes, and her curly auburn hair was left loose and flowing around her face.

When Todd met her eyes again, he looked surprised. "Wow," he said. "You look . . . great."

In keeping with her "Don't Scare Todd Off" plan, Alexandra grinned easily and pulled the door shut behind her. "What do I usually look like? Chopped liver?" she asked saucily as she led the way to Todd's car.

"No, no, it's just that . . ." Todd floundered as he hurried to open the passenger door.

"So did you have a good Christmas?" Alexandra said, letting him off the hook. She'd seen the look in his eyes—that was good enough.

"I think 'good' would be putting it a little

205

strong," he said dryly, starting the engine.

Alexandra laughed. "Well, let's just try to have a good time tonight. We'll eat, we'll dance, we'll—"

"Not drink," Todd supplied.

"Right!" Alexandra smiled at him in the dark confines of his car. He looked really great, she thought, suddenly feeling buoyant and happy. Tonight was going to be very interesting.

Hand in hand, Elizabeth and Tom walked through the wide double doors of the Sweet Valley High gymnasium. The interior had been completely decorated in Christmas colors, with red, green, and white streamers, large foil ornaments hanging from the ceiling, and red, green, and white balloons. Elizabeth knew that the decorations had been put up for the high school's Christmas dance only a few days before.

She felt a wave of nostalgia. Just last year she had blown up balloons for days for her senior-year Christmas dance. Coming into the gym, seeing it looking so familiar, was oddly bittersweet. For a moment she had the sudden longing simply to step backward in time, and to be arriving now for that same Christmas dance.

Then Tom squeezed her hand, and she looked up in surprise. What was she thinking? Of course she didn't want to go back in time. As painful as last semester had been sometimes, it was over now, and it had left her with a huge bonus: Tom, the man she loved.

Right now he was by her side, looking tall and handsome in his jacket and tie. In the parking lot after they'd arrived, they had lingered for long moments, kissing in the darkness of the car. Now his hair was still a little rumpled, and Elizabeth smoothed it.

"Elizabeth!" Olivia Davidson ran up and hugged her.

"Olivia—it's good to see you again!" Turning to Tom, she said, "Tom Watts, this is Olivia Davidson. Olivia and I used to work on the Sweet Valley *Oracle* together. This is my boyfriend, Tom."

"Good to meet you," Olivia said with a big smile. "Did you just get here? Doesn't the place look great?"

Talking happily, she led Elizabeth and Tom over to the refreshments table. "I'm so glad they decided to have a reunion right away," she said, helping herself to some cookies. "I've only been gone four months, but it feels like forever!"

"Tell me all about San Francisco," Elizabeth demanded. "How are your classes? Do you live on campus?"

Olivia laughed and began to answer her questions. Just then Annie Whitman and Cheryl Thomas ran up, their arms open for hugs.

After being introduced, Tom found himself standing to one side of a chattering gaggle of girls. It was a little awkward, but at the same time, he was glad to see Elizabeth so happy and animated. It was almost hard to believe this was his girlfriend. She'd had such a hard time finding a niche for herself at SVU, but here it was clear that she was in her element. She looked comfortable, at ease, and totally thrilled to be there. Tom decided to edge over to the drinks table and get some punch. With all her old friends swarming around Elizabeth, he felt decidedly superfluous.

"Lila, this is James Montgomery. James, this is my best friend, Lila Fowler." Proudly Jessica showed off her two favorite people. She knew heads had turned as soon as she and James had walked in, and she was having a blast being seen with him. He was definitely Greek-god material. As soon as she'd become aware of the jealous looks and knowing smiles people were sending her way, she'd felt right at home.

"Hi, James. You're a good sport for coming to this thing. Heck, I feel *I'm* a good sport to be here, and I actually *went* to Sweet Valley High!" Lila gave James a flirty look, and Jessica giggled tolerantly. The old Lila Fowler was definitely back.

"Oh, I'm having a great time," James said. "After all, I'm here with the most beautiful girl. So far three different guys have sent me looks to kill."

"Who?" Jessica cried excitedly, gazing around.

James laughed and held Jessica closely. "Forget it," he said. "You're here with me."

Laughing, Lila took a sip of her drink. So far, this reunion was going OK. Jessica was there, and that was fun. And Lila was looking forward to the fireworks when Elizabeth noticed that Alexandra Rollins was hanging on to Todd as if she were a desert and he was the last diet Pepsi. Lila had put money on a public display, but Jessica's five bucks insisted they would take it outside. Time would tell.

The band started playing a song, one of the same songs they had played last year at the senior prom, and people moved aside so that couples could start dancing. Heading backward, Lila bumped into a hard chest.

"Whoa!" Bruce said, stepping back quickly so his drink wouldn't spill on her. "Throwing yourself at me, Fowler?"

Lila made a face. "You wish. Why are you even here? Your reunion was last year."

Bruce grinned and licked his fingers where his drink had sloshed over. "I'm here in an official capacity," he informed her grandly. "I'm thinking about unloading a tax deduction on this dump, maybe setting up the Bruce Patman memorial volleyball court." He smirked. "What about you—enjoying yourself? Getting into the reunionizing spirit?"

"I'm trying," Lila said brightly.

A flicker of acknowledgment flashed momentarily across Bruce's blue eyes, and Lila realized with a little shock that of course he knew she'd been married, and that her husband was dead. He was just about the only person who'd never said anything about it one way or the other. Lila supposed it was just supreme self-absorption on his part, but whatever the reason, she was grateful.

"Yeah, well, this joint should be good for a couple laughs," Bruce said casually, taking a sip of his drink. A slight fragrance of alcohol drifted into the air, and Lila's nose tingled.

"Bruce, what are you drinking?" she demanded.

His eyes glittered. "Worried about me? I'm not a lush," he assured her. "I just thought a little bubbly would help get me through this."

"You have champagne?"

"Want some?" He smiled a challenge.

Lila was torn between having a lovely little sip of what she knew would be fabulous and expensive champagne, and having to endure Bruce's presence long enough to get it. "Where is it?" she asked cautiously.

A look of surprise crossed Bruce's face and just as quickly was extinguished. Then he leered wolfishly, but Lila had seen him in action for years and wasn't impressed. "Right this way, little girl," he said softly, motioning toward the door to the outside.

"Fine, let's go," she said brashly, heading through the crowd.

"Oh, Tom—there you are. Thought I'd lost you for a moment," Elizabeth said brightly, taking him by the arm. The band started playing a slow song, and she led him to the middle of the dance floor. Then he took her in his embrace, and she drifted against him, feeling blissfully happy. It was a perfect blending of old and new, she thought.

She was in one of her favorite places, surrounded by everyone she cared about, and yet Tom was with her too. Perfect.

She knew that everyone's eyes were on them as they swayed and turned slowly on the dance floor. From the first moment they'd walked into the gym, she knew that every old friend and vague acquaintance had measured Tom against Todd. Was he as tall? As good-looking? As athletic?

And though she knew the answers to all those questions were definitely yes, yes, and yes, none of it mattered. She knew what love was now. Love was not caring what other people thought. Love was being lost in your own world.

Elizabeth lifted her face, looking up at Tom. He gazed down at her, his smoky eyes glistening with love and admiration.

"Have I told you yet that you're the most beautiful girl I've ever known?" he said softly into her ear.

Elizabeth smiled. "If you really think so, then why aren't you kissing me?"

Smiling, Tom lowered his head and pressed his lips to hers. His mouth was warm, comforting, and exciting at the same time. Feeling daring, Elizabeth kissed him deeply. Time had moved on since her senior Christmas dance, and she had changed. It was time everyone knew about it.

Elizabeth tangled her fingers in Tom's thick brown hair, giving herself up to him, pressing against him, her body becoming one with his as the gym heated up with the warmth of hundreds of dancing bodies.

Pulling back a little, Elizabeth murmured, "Have I told you yet how great you've been at my parents' house? With all the commotion going on, I may have forgotten. But I've been very proud of you. And my parents love you."

"I did the best I could," Tom said smugly, holding her close.

Twenty minutes later Elizabeth excused herself to go to the ladies' room while Tom went to get them both some punch.

It took her a while to leave the gym, since she had to stop and talk to everyone she knew. Of course, quite a few of her classmates attended Sweet Valley University, like her, but so many had gone farther away to school. It was great to get caught up. Finally she made her way to the doors leading to the locker rooms.

In the hallway she was met with a familiar, musty smell. It was the smell of old basketball games, old laughter, old times. The past. For a second Elizabeth thought she could almost see Todd emerging from the dark of the boys' locker room, his brown hair still wet from a postgame shower, a faded purple T-shirt accentuating his well-developed chest and shoulders. And just as if he were really there, Elizabeth's heart skipped a beat, and she felt as giddy and love-struck as when she had first started dating the wonderful and strong Todd Wilkins.

212

What was wrong with her? She shook her head and went into the girls' bathroom. She stood in front of the mirror, looking at her reflection. Quickly she washed her hands, feeling as if she were washing the nostalgia for Todd away. When she looked up again, all she could think of was a future with Tom. *I'm glad I've moved on.*

The door opened behind her, and she was joined by Terri Adams, who had gone on a few double dates with her and Todd in high school, because her boyfriend had been Todd's friend and SVH's quarterback, Ken Matthews. Soon they were laughing and talking, and Elizabeth felt her weird nostalgia slip away.

Todd had seen Elizabeth slip away to the locker room, and he had swiveled Alexandra gently to watch her. He didn't know what kind of stunt she thought she was pulling, crawling over Watts like that in front of everyone. Just watching them had practically made Todd sick. *OK, Liz, I get the point. Quit hitting me over the head with it.*

Just last year he had been dancing to this song with Elizabeth. Alexandra tilted her head up to him and smiled, and he smiled back, unsure if it looked sincere. Sighing, he felt Alexandra tighten her hold around his waist, and obediently he moved closer. Alex was a nice girl. He knew she'd been lonely since Mark had gone to L.A. And God knew he was lonely, and full of missing Elizabeth. There was nothing wrong with their hanging out

213

together, though he knew they were exciting lots of gossip. Everyone could see that Alexandra and Elizabeth weren't speaking to each other. Probably some people, the ones who didn't know the real story, thought Todd had dumped Elizabeth for Alexandra.

He almost snorted in annoyance but stopped himself just in time. Probably not too cool to snort into your date's hair, he reminded himself. *Is she my date? We're here together. But is it a date?* He didn't know. Alexandra seemed to be comfortable hanging on to him. He guessed he was comfortable with it too, sort of. Or, he amended bitterly, as comfortable as he could be with his ex-girlfriend's ex–best friend hanging on to him in front of his ex-girlfriend and her new boyfriend. Whom he hated.

A flash of golden hair caught his eye, and he inconspicuously turned his feet to follow it. It was Elizabeth, heading back toward Watts, who was standing with Jessica and Jessica's new victim. Todd's gut tightened as Watts casually draped an arm around Elizabeth's waist and she leaned lovingly against him. Jessica's date and Watts were laughing, and Elizabeth was laughing too, her eyes wandering around the room.

A pain pierced his heart as her eyes locked on to his, and he saw her laugh fade. He remembered he was slow-dancing with Alexandra. He leaned away a little, and Alexandra looked up at him. She really did look pretty tonight, he thought. And she was

214

there, in his arms, not across the room staring at him as if he were a stranger. Smiling, he lowered his head to hers, noting her momentary surprise and then the flush of pleasure in her face as he began to kiss her. *Two can play at that game, Elizabeth,* he thought, deepening the kiss. Alexandra whimpered slightly against him, and he remembered when they had been lying on her bed at school, making out in an alcoholic daze. Well, he wasn't drunk now, and she felt great.

Ending the kiss, he looked up to see Elizabeth staring at him in shock, her mouth slightly open, her face pale. He felt a mean rush of triumph. Good. Let her be hurt. Maybe now she knew how he felt all the time. She'd been treating him as if he had no feelings at all. Now she'd know that he did, in fact, feel, and that those feelings were directed toward someone else.

"Todd—" Alexandra whispered dreamily, resting her head against him. Her shiny auburn hair waved around her face like a halo. "What was that for?"

"It was for you," he said in a low voice. "Because you're you. You're Alexandra."

When she looked up at him, her green eyes misty with happy tears, he felt like a total jerk.

"Could you excuse me, please?" Elizabeth said brittlely. "I think I need a bit of air."

"I'll come with you," Tom offered immediately.

"No, that's OK," she said firmly. "You stay

here. I'll just be a moment." Before he could protest, she slipped through the crowd and outside into the football field behind the school. Then she leaned against the building, her heart pounding, her breath coming in little gasps. Wildly, she felt that her and Todd's whole relationship had been a lie. Why was everything so painful sometimes? Why did life have to hurt?

Chapter Eighteen

"Umm, Cristal," Lila said appreciatively, taking another tiny sip of the champagne and letting the bubbles cascade down her throat. "Lovely."

"That's what I like," Bruce said. "A girl who enjoys the finer things in life."

Lila made a wry face. "Let's face it, Bruce. What you like is a girl who breathes."

Bruce laughed, showing even white teeth. "It's refreshing being around you, Li," he said. "It's been so easy knocking the SVU freshmen babes off their roosts that I'm bored with it. You can be a total pain in the butt, but you're not boring."

Lila grinned despite herself. "Thanks, I think." She took another tiny sip of champagne.

"So. You inherit a bundle from the count?" Bruce said baldly.

In other circumstances Lila would have felt a white-hot pain sear through her at the mention of Tisiano. But in this place, at this time, with Bruce, she found his audacious question merely amusing. Glancing over at him, she thought that Bruce somehow understood what no else did—that sometimes the pain was so bad that it was a relief to pretend not to care.

"Yep," she agreed lightly. "Tons. I have a castle in Italy I need to unload. You interested?"

"In the castle? No." Bruce smiled.

Lila took the last sip of her champagne. "I heard your bank account recently swelled, too."

"That's not the only thing, baby."

At the automatic and unthinking typical Bruce Patman response, Lila burst into laughter, and Bruce joined her. *If I didn't know better,* she thought, wiping her eyes, *I would almost say I'm having fun.*

Back inside, Elizabeth stood talking to Penny Ayala while people danced to a fast song. Tom had been commandeered by Winston Egbert, who of course knew him from SVU. They'd promised to be back in a few minutes.

Although she was smiling and chatting with Penny, Elizabeth still felt upset about Todd kissing Alexandra. She wasn't sure why—OK, so they were a couple. So what? Everyone was obviously seeing her and Tom as a couple; why did she care what Todd did? She didn't. Not at all.

"Hi, Elizabeth, Penny," Todd said, startling Elizabeth with his sudden appearance. He smiled at both of them, then gestured to the decorations.

"You think they just pulled out all the stuff we used last year, or did Chrome Dome Cooper spring for something new?"

Penny laughed and looked around. "Now that you mention it, I think I do recognize the large plastic Santa over there. Liz, do you remember how we almost killed ourselves last year, trying to get all the decorations finished in time for the dance?"

Elizabeth forced a smile. *Todd seems so normal. Just minutes ago he was looking at me like he hated me.* "Yeah."

Penny's eyes almost closed with laughter. "And we kept saying, 'Oh, God, we have to get home, we have to do our hair for the dance!' It was so funny."

"It really was," Elizabeth agreed. *I wanted to look my best for Todd.*

The band started a slow song, and Elizabeth looked around anxiously for Tom. He was nowhere to be seen.

"Elizabeth," Todd said evenly, "how about one for old times' sake?" He held out his hand.

She couldn't read the look in his eyes. Aware that Penny was staring at her, and that other people had heard Todd's question and were eagerly awaiting her response, Elizabeth felt herself grow defiant.

"Sure, Todd," she said calmly, walking toward the dance floor. "That would be nice."

In the middle of the dance floor, Todd took

219

her wordlessly into his arms. At first Elizabeth held herself stiffly away from him, her cheeks burning with the knowledge that everyone was watching them. Then Ken Matthews danced by with Olivia, and Olivia smiled at her understandingly. It made Elizabeth feel a little better.

"So" she murmured. "I guess you and Alexandra are boyfriend and girlfriend now."

"I don't want to talk about it," Todd said gently. "I just want to dance with you."

Elizabeth felt sad at hearing the tone in his voice. Almost as if they were still going out, but were just making up after an awful fight, she relaxed a little against him. He held her a little more tightly, but it felt OK. This was Todd. She trusted him. Looking around, Elizabeth found herself in a sea of happy laughter and familiar faces. Slowly, a comfortable smile spread across her face. A feeling filled her soul, a feeling so familiar she didn't even need to ask what it was. Suddenly, in her mind, she imagined that it wasn't December but last June, and she and Todd were a couple, they'd loved each other for what felt like ages, and they had nothing but a bright future ahead of them—a future *together*. Everyone thought so. *They* thought so.

It was really nice, she thought dreamily. Once she had been so happy with Todd, had assumed they would be together forever. No one had told her how short forever could be sometimes. And then, tonight, seeing him kiss Alexandra had been such a shock. Of course, she knew that he had done even more with Lauren Hill. When she'd found out about that, she'd literally thrown up. Shaking her head, she tried to put those thoughts out of her mind. They were together now, for old times' sake. That's all that mattered. Gently she rested her head against his chest and felt his sigh of contentment. He put his chin against her hair, just as he used to, and she felt a little thrill run down her spine.

"This is going to be good," Lila said, her brown eyes narrowed as she watched Elizabeth and Todd dancing closely on the dance floor.

"I hope she knows what she's doing," Jessica said worriedly. "Tom hasn't impressed me as the most tolerant guy in the world. Especially when it comes to Todd."

"Maybe we should increase the bet," Lila suggested. "I just saw Tom come inside with Winston."

"Lila!" Jessica frowned at her best friend. "This isn't just a bet—she's my sister. I'm watching a disaster in the making, and all you can think about is money?"

"Sorry, Jess," Lila said contritely.

"Besides," Jessica snapped, "all I have is five dollars. Take it or leave it."

From her seat on the bleachers, Alexandra watched the drama unfold. A tight, burning sense of anger coiled in her stomach and threatened to choke her. *Dammit! Why can't she leave him alone?* The evening had been going so well until now. Todd had been fairly attentive, and then there had been that searing kiss on the dance floor. They'd really been making progress. Everyone had been sending admiring glances Alexandra's way, and she had been happy and proud. For once she had really felt as if the old nerdy Enid had disappeared, and that the glamorous new Alexandra was firmly in place. And now look what had happened. Elizabeth was making a play for Todd right in front of everyone.

It was disgusting. She already had a boyfriend—did she think she could have them both? Watching Elizabeth's golden hair swaying back and forth, and seeing how Todd's eyes were closed blissfully, Alexandra felt overwhelmed with anger. *She always gets everything she wants,* Alexandra thought furiously. *She always has, and she always will. And until now I've always stood to one side and applauded. But no more. I'm not going to take this lying down, Elizabeth Wakefield. You've got Tom Watts eating out of your hand, and you're still trying to dangle Todd like a puppet on a string. But I'm going to fight you on this,* Alexandra swore. *I'm going to fight you, and I'm going to win. Wait and see.*

Her face contorted with the violence of her emotions, Alexandra stalked out of the gym.

*   *   *

222

Elizabeth drew in a deep, contented sigh. *Tom,* she thought. Her eyes flicked open. It wasn't Tom who was holding her, it was Todd. Elizabeth shook her head to clear it. Where was Tom? She missed him. With no warning Elizabeth found herself back in the present, and she was uncomfortable. *It's Tom I love!* she thought. *It's not high school anymore. It's not last June. It's December, it's my new life. And Tom is the one I love.* Her eyes lifted and she searched the crowd for Tom. There he was. At the edge of the dance floor, Tom was looking at her, his face filled with confusion and hurt. *What have I done?* She tried to make a reassuring face at him, but he turned on his heel and walked away. *I'd better go after him,* she thought, pressing on Todd's chest to get away.

"Todd, I'd better go," Elizabeth said apologetically.

But he wouldn't let her leave. His arms were around her waist, and he tightened them.

Looking up at him in surprise, Elizabeth repeated, "Todd—please. I'd better go after Tom."

But Todd merely looked down at her. "Liz, for God's sake, one lousy dance. Is that too much to ask? Watts can wait. Don't you get it? I love you. I've always loved you, I will always love you. When are you going to admit you feel the same way?" He tightened his grip on her still further, pressing his body against hers from shoulder to knee.

Elizabeth's eyes narrowed. "I can't believe this. *You* dumped *me,* remember?"

A look of pain clouded Todd's eyes. "It was the stupidest thing I've ever done," he admitted. "All I can do is beg your forgiveness and promise I'll try to make it up to you. I need you, Elizabeth," he pleaded. "Everything in my life has gone downhill since we broke up. If we were back together, I know it would all be OK again."

"No, Todd!" Elizabeth cried, pushing against him. "Tom is my boyfriend now, and Alexandra is your girlfriend! Now, let me go!" Around them people were staring, watching their struggle.

Elizabeth was about to call for help when a voice said, "May I cut in?" Tom thumped Todd's shoulder, hard.

"Get lost," Todd said angrily.

"Tom!" Elizabeth cried, pushing against Todd. "Help me."

Their old classmates gathered around them. It was just the three of them in a circle of concerned faces.

"Leave her alone," Tom said, trying to pry Todd's arm away from Elizabeth's shoulder.

Todd let the arm fly, sending Tom stumbling backward. Tom shrugged his jacket back into place, his face determined. When he spoke, his voice was even and cool.

"Don't you see she doesn't want to be with you anymore, Wilkins?" he said flatly.

"All I see is Elizabeth in my arms, Watts," Todd snarled.

"She's not a *thing*, Todd. You can't just have her because you want her. Go ahead. Ask her what she wants."

Todd suddenly looked confused—and scared.

"Here, ask her yourself!" he cried, shoving Elizabeth away, sending her reeling so that she almost fell. Jessica ran up next to her and caught her.

"Oh, Jess," she gasped. "I don't believe this is happening!"

"That's it!" Tom snarled, throwing his suit jacket to the ground.

The two faced off, ducking and turning, cocking their fists.

Murmuring worriedly, everyone pushed back to give them room.

"No, stop it!" Elizabeth cried, but they both ignored her.

Then Todd lunged and landed a blow against Tom's chest, sending him backward. Before Tom could regain his balance, Todd was all over him, punching him with blows fueled by anger and jealousy.

But Tom ducked and parried, taking some punches but throwing plenty of his own. As an ex–football player, he still had a somewhat heavier build than Todd, and within thirty seconds it became clear that he was packing more power behind his punches.

Her face a mask of horror, Elizabeth clung to Jessica at the edge of the crowd. Dimly she was aware of Alexandra pushing her way to the front of the crowd. Elizabeth felt shocked by the expression on her face. Instead of worry or fear, Alexandra was staring at the two fighters with what looked like hatred. Then her eyes flicked up to Elizabeth, and they narrowed. Elizabeth felt a chill run down her back. *That can't be Alexandra, looking at me like that. What have I done?*

Tiring, Todd got knocked off balance by a punch in his stomach, and his breath came out in a "whoof!" Then Tom, his face cold and damp with sweat, stepped closer and cracked a heavy right against Todd's jaw. Todd spun away, his eyes open in surprise. Blood started running from his lip, and he put up his hand in disbelief.

"Tom, no!" Elizabeth said, in tears now.

But Tom relentlessly followed Todd and cracked him again with an uppercut beneath the chin. Todd's head snapped back, and a spray of blood arced through the air in heavy red drops. Everyone surged back, silent. Todd's knees buckled, his eyes fluttered. Then he pitched backward, blood streaming from his nose and mouth, and landed flat on his back. He lifted his head once, groaned, then let it fall to the floor with a thud. His eyes were closed. He didn't move.

The crowd was completely still for a moment, then broke into action.

Tom was still standing, bruises already darkening on his face. He was breathing hard, and his shirt was wet with sweat and spotted with Todd's blood. Bringing one arm up, he wiped his face, his eyes not leaving Elizabeth.

"Oh, Todd," she wailed; then, with a concerned look, she bolted forward and instinctively knelt beside him. "Someone call an ambulance," she wept, brushing Todd's hair off his face. He was still out cold, and his blood was running down the side of his face to the floor. Someone tossed her a handkerchief, and she held it to Todd's nose to try to stop the bleeding. She looked up at Tom again to plead for help, but he was nowhere to be seen.

When she looked down at Todd again, his eyes were fluttering. Elizabeth felt a hot anger building inside her. "You're so stupid!" she hissed. "You've ruined everything! You better get some help before you ruin your whole life! I'm never coming back to you—never!"

Her fists clenched, Elizabeth stood. Alexandra was standing close by, a mix of emotions on her face. Elizabeth grabbed Alexandra's hand and yanked her over to where Todd lay.

"Here," Elizabeth snapped. "He's your problem now."

Then she turned and ran, pushing her way through the crowd. She heard Jessica calling her but kept going, her eyes searching frantically for Tom.

"Let him go, Liz!" she heard someone yell.

"No!" she cried. "Tom, Tom, wait!"

But she couldn't find him anywhere. Tears running down her face, she searched both locker rooms, the shadows under the bleachers, everywhere.

"Tom!" she screamed. When she saw the door leading outside, she dashed for the exit.

A sole figure was walking between the parked cars, through the pools of blue streetlight.

"Tom!" Elizabeth cried into the night.

Tom stopped in his tracks, but he didn't turn around. Then he kept walking.

Elizabeth ran down the steps, cursing her high heels, and through the darkened cars. When she caught up to him, she threw her arms around him from the back, sobbing, holding on tight.

"Don't you leave me!" she cried angrily. "Don't you dare!" She didn't know what had come over her—in the last few minutes she had felt stronger emotions than she had ever felt before. But all she knew now was that if Tom left her, she would be distraught. She refused to allow it. Still she clung to him, crying against his broad back.

Slowly he turned in her arms and looked down at her. "It looked like you wanted me to leave," he said.

"Well, I don't! So forget about it!" Then she leaned against his chest and held him tightly. Tomorrow she would have to figure out this uncharacteristic behavior, but for tonight she was going to fight for the man she loved. Tom stroked her hair and held her close, and she shuddered in his embrace. Minutes later her crying quieted.

"Tom, don't you know that it's you I love?" Elizabeth said. "You, you, and only you."

"Are you sure?" Tom breathed, a hopeful look

coming into his eye. "Even after all that?"

Elizabeth reached up and tenderly kissed his cut lip. "Even after anything. Now—and forever," she said, taking him by the hand and leading him out of the streetlight and into the shadows of the night.

"Elizabeth OK?" Lila asked concernedly as Jessica came up holding her leather jacket.

"Yeah." Jessica tugged her long hair out from her collar and zipped it up. "I saw her leave with Tom. Guess they'll go make up somewhere."

"Oh, good." Lila's face cleared and she held out her hand. "It was public. Pay up."

"OK, OK." Grumpily Jessica fished in her purse and then slammed a crumpled five-dollar bill into Lila's hand. Lila grinned.

"Now what?" Lila asked.

Jessica's face brightened. "James and I are taking off. I thought I might show him the hot spots of Sweet Valley—like the beach, Miller's Point . . ."

Lila giggled. "Have a good time. I'm going to head on home, I guess. Call me tomorrow, OK? Maybe we can get together."

"Promise," Jessica said. Then James came up and she gave him a dazzling smile. "Later, Lila." Taking James's arm, she headed him toward the exit. "And I bet you thought nothing exciting ever happened in Sweet Valley," she cooed as they pushed through the doors.

James smiled, giving his Greek-god impression.

"I sure don't think that anymore. Is your sister OK?"

Jessica nodded. "She'll be fine." When James opened the passenger-side door of his Miata, she slid in, grateful to sit down and relax after the harrowing last half hour.

He joined her in the car and reached out to smooth her hair back. "I still had a great time with you tonight," he said. "Even if things did get a little out of hand. You were the most beautiful girl there."

Jessica smiled demurely. "Thank you. I thought you were the hottest guy there too."

James started the engine. "Are you tired? Should I take you home?"

"Actually," Jessica said, "I was wondering if you wanted to go somewhere to be alone for a while." She smiled innocently. "It would give us a chance to relax after all the excitement."

In the darkness James's green eyes glittered, and he leaned over to capture her lips in a brief kiss. "Sounds good to me. Just point me in the right direction."

Giggling, Jessica pointed toward the road to the beach. "That way, James."

Here's a sneak preview of Sweet Valley University #9, Sorority Scandal, *coming to bookstores in February.*

Two weeks later . . .

Lila stood on the tarmac at the small local airport.

"What's wrong with the plane?" she demanded. The chilly night air whipped her long brown hair, and she tightened the silk scarf inside the collar of her leather flight jacket.

The mechanic looked at her apologetically. "I'm sorry, miss. No one told me you'd rented this plane for tonight. We've just taken the engine apart."

"But I called this afternoon!" Lila fumed. It was a Friday night. In another week her classes would start at Sweet Valley University, and she was looking forward to them. As she had planned, she'd found an apartment to rent, close to the university. It was a large two-bedroom penthouse at the top of a luxurious condominium building. From her living-room window she could see almost as far as Sweet Valley.

All day she and her mother had been shopping

for household stuff, since she'd brought almost nothing back from Italy. But tonight she'd been bored. Jessica had been on a date with James, and no one else really seemed fun to hang out with. Instead of moping in her room by herself, she'd decided to go flying by herself instead. It was high time she put her nightmares to rest for good, and flying and safely landing her plane would do that. But now her plane wasn't available. It was infuriating. Gritting her teeth, she resigned herself to a long night of channel-surfing.

"What's the matter, Fowler? The rubber band on your propeller break?"

Whirling, Lila faced Bruce's handsome, sneering face. *Great. Just what I need.* Since their temporary truce at the reunion, Lila had seen Bruce only once. It had been at the Dairi Burger, when Lila was with Jessica, and Bruce had been so obnoxious that it hadn't even been funny. All of her slightly more charitable ideas about him had been wiped clean. "They're overhauling the engine," she informed him coldly. "What about you? Get stood up tonight? I didn't think the kind of girls you dated did that. After all, if you don't have enough cash, they probably take Visa."

Bruce snorted. "Very funny. For your information, girls would be happy to pay *me*. In fact, now that I think about it, you're about the only person around who could afford my favors."

Lila almost laughed. Bruce elevated arrogance to an art form.

232

Then Bruce cracked a smile. "What say we take a little spin, Fowler?" He jerked his head to where a small bright-red Cessna was waiting by the open hangar door. "It's a beautiful night," he coaxed. "I'll even let you touch my . . . throttle."

Lila grimaced. "I'll throttle you, all right," she said sweetly, and he laughed.

"No, seriously. Let's both ditch this lame town and hit the skies. Come on. You got nothing better to do," he said knowledgeably.

Lila actually considered it for a moment. She'd had her heart set on getting far above the city, far above her memories. And it would be satisfying to show Bruce just how good a pilot she was. Then she could forget about her nightmare once and for all.

"Well, OK," she said less than graciously. "Let's go."

Two weeks have passed since that fateful night at the Sweet Valley High reunion. What have Elizabeth and Jessica been doing? Read Sweet Valley University Thriller Edition #1, Wanted for Murder, *and find out!*

SIGN UP FOR THE SWEET VALLEY HIGH® FAN CLUB!

Hey, girls! Get all the gossip on Sweet Valley High's® most popular teenagers when you join our fantastic Fan Club! As a member, you'll get all of this really cool stuff:

- Membership Card with your own personal Fan Club ID number
- A Sweet Valley High® Secret Treasure Box
- Sweet Valley High® Stationery
- Official Fan Club Pencil (for secret note writing!)
- Three Bookmarks
- A "Members Only" Door Hanger
- Two Skeins of J. & P. Coats® Embroidery Floss with flower barrette instruction leaflet
- Two editions of *The Oracle* newsletter
- Plus exclusive Sweet Valley High® product offers, special savings, contests, and much more!

Be the first to find out what Jessica & Elizabeth Wakefield are up to by joining the Sweet Valley High® Fan Club for the one-year membership fee of only $6.25 each for U.S. residents, $8.25 for Canadian residents (U.S. currency). Includes shipping & handling.

Send a check or money order (do not send cash) made payable to "Sweet Valley High® Fan Club" along with this form to:

SWEET VALLEY HIGH® FAN CLUB, BOX 3919-B, SCHAUMBURG, IL 60168-3919

NAME_____
(Please print clearly)

ADDRESS_____

CITY_____ STATE _____ ZIP_____
(Required)

AGE_____ BIRTHDAY_____ /_____ /_____

Offer good while supplies last. Allow 6-8 weeks after check clearance for delivery. Addresses without ZIP codes cannot be honored. Offer good in USA & Canada only. Void where prohibited by law.
©1993 by Francine Pascal   LCI-1383-123